Hitched

Volume 2

Kendall Ryan

Hitched (Volume Two)

Copyright © 2016 Kendall Ryan

Developmental Editing by
Alexandra Fresch

Copy Editing and Formatting by
Pam Berehulke

Cover design by
Hang Le

About the Book

Arranged marriage? Check.

Cocky new husband? Check.

It's a marriage of convenience—one I'm determined to keep strictly professional. I can't be stupid enough to fall for this sexy playboy's charm or advances. I have to be strong, even if he is my husband.

Except he has a huge cock with an even bigger ego, and his main goal in life seems to be getting me to stroke both. The arrogant bastard is like sweet, sugary candy for my libido. I know he's bad for me.

But I want to devour every wicked inch of him.

With his sexual prowess and experience, I know he'll be explosive in the bedroom. And since we're stuck together for the foreseeable future—keeping up this marriage charade long enough to turn the company profitable again—I deserve something to look forward to at the end of a long workday, right?

What could one little taste hurt?

Praise for *Hitched*

"I'm literally in love with *Hitched*. The irreverent humor, fun storyline and intriguing characters enchanted me immediately and I was hooked. I mean really, when a book has a chapter with only the two words being "Game on" (right after the chapter where Noah pulls his big boy parts out in a swanky bar) you know this is going to be a fun and funny read! And Ms. Ryan didn't disappoint . . . she kept me cracking up the entire read! I'm salivating for the next installment!"

—The Romance Reviews

"Fun, flirty and steamy, *Hitched* will have you addicted from the first word! Kendall Ryan delivered big time, I'm practically salivating for more!" *—Angie and Jessica's Dreamy Reads*

"Kendall Ryan strikes gold in her latest super star, *Hitched*, a romantic comedy spiked with steam, anchored by angst, and flooded with feelings."

—Bookalicious Babes Blog

"Charming, swoony and playful, Kendall Ryan's *Hitched* left me salivating for more. More Noah, more Olivia, more of this series which already has my heart all aflutter, my smile perma-pinned to my face, and my mind aching for answers."

—Give Me Books

"*Hitched* was a perfect non-stop read! I read it in one sitting, and laughed so many times my belly ached. It's a fun, romantic read with a light-hearted story that made me ache for more when I finished."

—Jacqueline's Reads

"*Hitched* will grab you hook, line, and sinker from the very first page. Olivia is a little bratty and Noah is a whole lot cocky but that dynamic makes for a sexual tension that I can tell is going to explode in the next two installments. And while this isn't your typical friends-to-lovers type of story, the shared history between the two adds a surprising depth. The steam level is heating up and once you pick it up, you won't want to put it down."

—*Love Between the Sheets*

Chapter One

Noah

What a fucking public relations nightmare.

I'm at a charity event on behalf of Tate & Cane Enterprises. My new *wife* hasn't been seen or heard from in two days; my best friend, Sterling, is in the bathroom fucking a waitress; and I'm standing here with a spatula in my hand, cursing them all a slow death under my breath.

We're at a charity event at a soup kitchen. Supposedly, we're doing good for the impoverished youths of our community, but it's really just an excuse to empty the pockets of New York's elite by serving them a very overpriced lunch. And considering I'm one of the cooks, I doubt it'll taste like much. I enjoy cooking; I just rarely do it. I have one, maybe two recipes my mother used to make that I've mastered, and curried chicken salad isn't one of them. The smell alone is nauseating. Though that could be because I have no appetite.

For the hundredth time, I wish I'd just hired Rosita and written her a blank check. If I had, they'd be eating like kings today. But the good cause isn't the only reason I'm here. Hell, it's not even my main reason.

As soon as I arrived at the soup kitchen this morning, the vultures of New York high society descended, peppering me with questions. How was the wedding? Why are you alone? Where's your blushing goddamned bride?

Even if I had a clue how to answer, it was none of their fucking business. Olivia's father, Fred Cane, stepped in and saved me, telling everyone the ceremony was intimate and beautiful, and that Olivia sends her regrets but was unable to make it. I volunteered for kitchen duty just to get a few hours of peace away from the public eye.

Or at least, that was the idea. I force myself to grin at the photographer who invaded the kitchen twenty minutes ago as his camera clicks away. If he asks me one more time where Olivia is, I'm going to shove his thousand-dollar camera up his ass.

"How's it coming?" the lead cook asks, looking

into the massive stainless steel mixing bowl of chopped chicken dripping in amber curry.

"All set." I slide the bowl toward him just as another cook sets a tray of pre-sliced croissants on the industrial kitchen's counter.

They thank me for coming today as I remove my stained apron and toss it in the laundry basket on my way out of the kitchen.

A few more hands to shake, a couple of photo ops, and then I'm out of here. Sterling is still nowhere to be found, but the prick can find his own ride home. It's not as if New York City isn't crawling with taxis. And I'm not in the mood for company anyway.

When Olivia stood me up at the altar, something inside me broke. I'd worked my ass off to try to show her that we could actually work as a couple, and I thought we were getting somewhere. Sharing an apartment, sleeping in the same bed, our sweet make-out sessions that were starting to turn into something more. And we were gelling at the office too . . . slowly turning the company around, one executive decision at a time.

I blow out a frustrated sigh. Never in my life have I worked this hard at winning over a woman. But Olivia's not just any woman. I grew up with her, placed her on this untouchable pedestal for twenty years, and she was *this close* to being mine. Before she ran off. And I still don't even understand why. Though I have a damn good idea—

The heir clause in our inheritance contract.

Sterling was right. I guess she didn't want me putting a bun in her oven after all. But I never thought she'd react like this. Scream and swear and cut off my balls, yes. Vanish without a trace, no.

In the event hall, people are mingling, shaking hands, and munching on the crudité. I spot Olivia's father at the far end of the room and start toward him. He's a short, squat man with silver hair, a round belly, and a perpetual grin on his face. Basically, he's like Santa's brother. It's hard not to love the guy, even when he won't tell me what I need to know, and is being a royal pain in my ass.

"You ready to tell me where she is?" I ask, leaning in so only he can hear me.

He excuses himself from the man he was talking to and turns toward me. "Noah," he starts, his tone jovial as if we're discussing our upcoming yachting weekend on the Hudson.

"Cut the shit, old man." I maintain a friendly grin in case anyone is watching. "Where is she?"

He lets out a heavy sigh, and for the first time, I can see that this is weighing on him almost as much as it's weighing on me.

"She's somewhere safe, that's all that matters, and she's mulling things over. She'll be back when she's ready. This is Olivia we're talking about."

I nod solemnly. She's as stubborn as the day is long. And he's right. She'll be back when she's good and ready. Probably with an iron-clad argument, ready to negotiate the terms of her uterus with gusto. I smirk at the thought. At first I figured she was staying with Camryn, but after ransacking her best friend's apartment, my new guess is one of Manhattan's five-star hotels.

"When you speak with her again, tell her to call

me," I hiss under my breath. Fred and I have always been on good terms—he was my father's closest friend, after all—but my patience has run thin.

He nods. "Of course I will."

Just then, Sterling approaches with that just-fucked look. You know the one. Mussed hair, wrinkled collar, shirt untucked, smug-ass grin on his face like he just got his nuts off. *The fucking bastard.*

"Well, that was quick." I check my watch. "If you need lessons in stamina, all you have to do is ask."

An elbow in the ribs kills my smile. "Fuck off, Noah. We both know why you're in a foul mood, and I don't blame you."

Fred excuses himself as Sterling and I trade jabs.

"So, was she fun?" I ask as we walk toward the exit.

"Of course," he replies. But his eyes are on the door and there's no conviction in his voice.

I've been there. Quick, unmemorable fucks with girls whose names I couldn't even recall a mere twenty-four hours later. Which is all the more reason why

Olivia's disappearing act feels like something had been ripped out of me.

Sure, we had our ups and downs, but I miss the banter, miss the way I could rile her up with the slightest of provocations. I just missed her.

I'm not looking forward to going home alone. The apartment feels stale without her. She hadn't even been there long, and already the place felt empty and void without her. Like all the warmth and charm has been sucked out by a vacuum. Only her scent lingers, and it makes me ache for her even more. Just when I started to get used to a woman's touch at home, it was all ripped away. And that damn teapot she got us as a housewarming gift sits unused on the kitchen counter, mocking me. Why give me a peace token if she was just going to run out on me?

Sinking down onto the vinyl backseat of a cab, I let out a sigh. I've been hounding Fred about where she is, but the truth is, I don't care. Well, I do care—every time I turn around and see she's not there, her absence hurts all over again. But what I really want is to know *why* she ran out on me. Left me standing on the beach like a fucking idiot, waiting for our ceremony to start.

My head is swimming with questions, with anger and confusion and loss, and there's an unexplained ache in my chest. It's eerily familiar. Almost like the relentless throbbing I felt when Mum died. The kind of pain that fades a fraction with each passing day, but never goes away completely.

"You okay, buddy?" the cab driver asks, peering at me in the rearview mirror.

"I'm fine. Sorry." Shit, I spaced out. I've been just sitting here in the back of his cab.

"You have somewhere you need to be?" he asks.

"Yes, home." I give him the address, bewildered about the fact that I've started thinking of our shared penthouse as *home*.

My phone rings. My heart rate kicks up—for a second, I wonder if it's Olivia. But the name flashing on my screen for the third time today quickly informs me otherwise.

"Hello?" I mumble, deflated.

"How are you holding up?" Rosita asks.

She's been calling every couple of hours, but this is the first time I've answered. Something about discussing it out loud—let alone with another person—might make this whole nightmare too real. But the sincerity in her tone is genuine and honest, and I suddenly feel like a dick for putting off her calls.

"I'm okay, I guess. Just confused."

She sighs, and I can imagine her nodding her head, agreeing with me.

"When I learned you were getting married, I wasn't sure what to think of this whole arrangement, but I figured if it was what your father wanted, it was for the best. He was a good man. And he loved both you and Olivia."

"Yeah," I say, agreeing with her. But in times like this, where everything seems so fucked, it makes it hard to figure out what Dad was thinking.

I hear a rush of static as Rosita takes a deep breath. "But the more I got to thinking about it all, I realized I liked the idea of you getting married. Someone to cook you breakfast in the morning, someone to make sure you're okay. A wife getting after you to make sure you take your vitamins. I liked the idea."

I chuckle at her. "I can take care of myself, you know?" Rosita's always been such a mother hen.

"I know, *hijo*," she replies without missing a beat. "I know you can. But I liked that you wouldn't have to."

"You do know I was left at the altar, right?" As sweet as her sentiment is, the timing is horrible. Besides, it's not like Olivia is the doting, domestic type, bringing me slippers and serving me breakfast in bed.

"Of course I do. What I'm saying is that even though your ego is bruised, you need to take a deep breath and figure out why she left. See if there's something you can do to fix this. Because I really think the two of you could work."

I swallow the boulder in my throat. The only time Rosita has really seen Olivia and me together was at her daughter Maria's birthday party. A rare smile graces my lips at the memory. It was a fun day. Navigating Rosita's enthusiastic extended family with my timid Snowflake by my side.

"I will listen to every word she says, I promise you that." Whenever Olivia gets around to coming back. *If* she comes back.

"Okay. Be good. Love you."

"Love you too, Rosie." I stuff my cell back in my pocket and hand a twenty to the cab driver as he rolls to a stop in front of our building.

Upstairs, I toss my keys in the wooden bowl by our penthouse door and wander inside. I'm really not looking forward to sleeping alone tonight. I consider heading back out, maybe to the bar down the street to drown my sorrows in a glass of fine whiskey. I flip on the light—and I freeze.

Olivia is sitting on the couch. Her hands are folded in her lap, and she looks tired. Her dark blond waves are disheveled and that glow in her cheeks is gone.

"I need your help," she says.

Has she been waiting for me? How long? And is *that* all she has to say? Four simple words . . . when four thousand wouldn't be enough. And she's asking for a favor?

My jaw tightens as disbelief darkens into anger.

"First, I need some answers," I demand.

Chapter Two

Olivia

I arrive back at the penthouse early in the afternoon. Noah's not here, so I change into fresh clothes and eat a granola bar while I wait. I lie down for a nap, but end up just staring at the ceiling; try to work, but stop because I can't focus; try to read a magazine, then resign myself to waiting on the sofa.

Where the hell is he? He wouldn't be at the office on a Sunday—this is Noah we're talking about. I try not to think about the possibility that he stayed the night with another woman.

But if he did . . . well, I'm the one who abandoned our wedding. I can't blame him for thinking our relationship is over. For wanting to be done with me, and find a new girlfriend who isn't such a hassle. Even though the last thing on my mind yesterday was hurting him.

God, the nightmare of the last forty-eight hours is

still spinning through my head. I can still hear Brad's voice on the phone, slithering into my ear like some horrible alien parasite . . .

• • •

"Good afternoon, Olivia," Brad said. "You really should check your e-mail more often."

"Wh-what do you want?" I choked out.

"Check your e-mail and tell me if you recognize the attached photos."

I hammered the END CALL icon and tapped my e-mail app. One new message. I opened it . . . and my breath froze solid in my throat.

Of course I recognized those pictures. Back when we were still dating, Brad had nagged me to take some sexy naked selfies for him. And I'd caved, because I was still a gullible girl who thought he might turn into a decent boyfriend if I just tried hard enough and gave him whatever his slimy, shriveled little heart desired.

He'd had me convinced that he was a good man and all his selfish, controlling behavior was my fault.

Whenever he was mad, it was because I'd provoked him. (Of course, when I was mad, I was just a childish bitch who looked for reasons to get offended.) He'd sulked when I didn't want to touch his boner; he'd sulked when I suggested he could maybe touch my clit once in a while. Even when I'd caught him flirting with other women, he'd claimed it was because I neglected him.

So I guess I shouldn't have put it past him to lie about destroying these nude pics either. I'd made him delete them off his phone while I watched, but he must have backed up the files somewhere beforehand. All twenty-two of them. *Fuck.*

I hit redial. Brad's phone didn't even finish one ring before he picked up.

"So?"

Squaring my jaw, I put on the hardest, most contemptuous tone I could. I refused to give him the satisfaction of hearing my voice shake. "Do you have some sort of point to make? Or did you just want to remind me what a scumbag you are?"

"Give up and let my father buy Tate & Cane," he demanded. "I could also ask you to get down on your knees and suck my dick, but we both know you're not even good for that much."

"Only because you always jammed it down my throat like you were drilling for oil. Or compensating for something."

"Do you want the deal or not?" he snapped.

Oh, Brad hadn't liked that. I could just imagine his curled lip. I felt a rush of simultaneous triumph and terror at having pissed him off.

"I'm afraid this is a limited-time offer. If you want to save Tate & Cane, have your board e-mail me a buyer's contract by the end of the week. Or I'll release these photos—destroying your reputation and probably your company's too—and then Daniels Multimedia Enterprises will just buy Tate & Cane anyway when its deadline is up. One way or another, my father will get what he wants."

My heart was hammering so hard, I could barely catch my breath. I tried to buy time to think by arguing with him, digging for any crack in his resolve. "Is this all about your dad? What are you getting out of this?"

"Being a good son is its own reward. As well as building a strong company to someday inherit . . . and seeing a snotty bitch get what she richly deserves." His tone impaled me like shards of ice as he went on. "Whatever explanation you prefer. Pick your favorite; it doesn't matter."

So that's what this was really about—punishing me for daring to break up with him. Even for Brad the Demon Ex, this was insane. I'd never dreamed he'd go so far for such petty revenge.

"What matters," he continued, "is your own decision. My offer is quite generous. I'm willing to pay millions of dollars for your company instead of just demanding you hand it over."

I swallowed. "You said I have one week?" I asked, hating how small and weak my voice sounded.

"That's right," he said, sounding pleased to have finally reined me in. "Good-bye for now, Olivia. We'll keep in touch."

At least, I thought that's what Brad had said. I couldn't hear over the rush of blood pounding in my ears. His last words could have been *you're fucked.*

And they might as well be. I stared down at my phone, wanting to cry and puke and scream all at the same time. What the fuck was I going to do? What *could* I do? No way out. I couldn't think straight. My already-simmering anxiety had boiled over. Animal panic flooded my brain. *Can't breathe. Trapped . . .*

Even then, part of me already knew I needed help. I should have asked Noah. But how could I possibly face him? I'd handed Brad the rope to hang us both with. I'd given him exactly what he needed to destroy our fathers' legacy and six thousand jobs.

Brad's toxic influence came roaring back full force, making me relive all the sick, distorted feelings that our relationship had ground into me for over two years. My vision clouded, my lungs burned, my stomach twisted with anxiety.

No, I couldn't tell Noah. The way he'd look at me . . . I didn't know which would be worse, his disappointment or his pity. My pride couldn't take another blow. I'd just shatter.

In that moment, I hated myself more than I'd hated anyone in my life. I was trembling with shame and helpless rage.

Why the hell did I ever take those pictures for Brad? I'd always let that scumbag use me, just rolled over and did whatever he wanted. If I hadn't been so naive and desperate, I wouldn't be in this mess right now. Why did it take me so long to hear the tiny voice in the back of my head screaming *this relationship is wrong, it's killing you, get out now?*

Well, I'd listened too late. And unless I did something right now, our whole company was going to pay for my mistake.

I had to find Brad and stop him, although I had no idea what I was going to do or say when I got to his office. My instincts just screamed that there was a threat and that I needed to meet it and fight and kill it, because if I stood still, it would find me and hurt me first. Letting it come to me would mean that I'd already lost.

Half-blind with adrenaline, I ran out of the cottage,

jumped into our rental car, and hauled ass for Nantucket's only airport. I had one thing on my mind: taking down Brad and making him pay.

Dark and frantic thoughts barreled through my brain. I'd been right all along to feel skittish about marrying Noah. If Brad was going to ruin our company no matter what I did, then what was the point? If this exploded into a media scandal, the best-case scenario was that I'd have to step down while the company carried on without me. In which case, the question of my inheritance was moot. I could already see the headline—"CEO Forced to Resign Amidst Nude Photo Scandal." Not how I wanted my first appearance on CNN to go down.

Nauseated, with tears stinging my eyes and still decked out in all my meaningless finery, I floored the gas pedal and left our wedding far behind.

The flight from Nantucket, as short as it was, still forced me to sit and think. I realized that I'd let my emotions run away with me—quite literally. How the hell was bolting supposed to fix anything? As satisfying as it would feel in the short term, I couldn't just barge into Brad's office and start screaming obscenities at him. No, I needed a plan before I acted.

I needed help too. But with my stomach still churning with anxiety and shame, I didn't want Noah to know about my dirty pictures—or about how much power Brad apparently still wielded over me.

So instead of meeting Brad, I took a cab to an Upper East Side hotel, promising myself that I could solve this problem alone, and nobody would find out what I'd done for Brad or what he'd done to me.

I just wanted to feel like I wasn't totally useless. I knew that stopping Brad wouldn't make up for the way I'd treated Noah that day, let alone justify it. But I figured that a victorious return was better than slinking back with my tail between my legs. It was bad enough that I'd betrayed my fiancé; I didn't want to dump all my problems into his lap too. I was determined to stay independent. I was Olivia Fucking Cane. I would find a way to fix this.

In the end, though, I couldn't keep inventing excuses to avoid Noah. I spent two sleepless nights pacing my hotel room, trying to brainstorm ways to defuse Brad's blackmail threat . . . and I came up with jack shit. Every idea was worse than the last. There was no way I could fight back without getting other people involved and drawing attention to my dirty little secret.

At sunrise today, I gave up and went to bed, where my mind kept spinning until I fell asleep from sheer exhaustion.

Later in the morning, as I stared into the mirror, I was forced to admit what I'd known all along. *I can't do this alone.* This mistake was too old and too deep to be undone easily—or maybe at all. And Brad's claws were sunk too deep in me. Just remembering his voice on the phone made my heart race and my stomach twist. I could barely think straight, and that asshole wasn't even here right now.

No, I had to face facts . . . and Noah too. So I took a shower and made my haggard face as presentable as I could. With nothing else to wear, I put on yesterday's clothes—what should have been my wedding dress. I went downstairs, ate a bagel without tasting anything, and took a paper cup of coffee from the continental breakfast bar, then called a cab to take me to our penthouse.

It was time to go home to my husband.

· · ·

The sound of the doorknob turning startles me out of my painful memories. I jolt upright and watch, my heart beating fast as our front door swings open.

Noah steps over the threshold . . . then sees me and freezes. He stares into my eyes like he's seen a ghost. Anger, relief, and hurt fight for control of his expression.

All my carefully rehearsed words desert me at the sight of him. My throat feels dry, and with my heart hammering, I utter the first words I can think of.

"I need your help."

For a minute he says nothing. He just keeps staring at me, fighting to school his features. Finally, he replies, "First, I need some answers."

His voice is tight, barely keeping control. But he didn't say *no*. That's about the best I could have hoped for—hell, the best I deserve. I nod and rise to my feet.

"Where the hell have you been?" he asks. He still hasn't moved from the door, as if he doesn't want to get too close to me.

"I'm sorry I left. I was at a hotel." I know that doesn't come close to answering his real question, but I have to start somewhere.

Noah slams the door shut and strides toward me. "Jesus Christ, Olivia. I thought you were gone for good. Why didn't you say anything?"

Biting my lip, I swallow hard. The pain in his voice is palpable. *I betrayed him . . . there's no other way to put it.*

His outrage keeps pouring out, burying me like an avalanche. "You left me standing at that altar for a fucking hour. I've never been so humiliated in my whole life. And I've been losing my mind ever since. We've had to lie our asses off to keep the media from suspecting anything, all while I had no idea where the fuck you were. I knew you didn't want to marry me, but for God's sake, I never thought you hated me this much."

The word feels like a cold needle in my heart. Hate

him? No, I don't, I couldn't . . . but that's exactly how I acted, wasn't it? Like I didn't consider him worthy of basic respect. How can I fault him for thinking that's how I felt?

Scowling, Noah cuts his hands through the air. "You abandoned me. Without a word. Without giving anyone a chance to do anything. I had no idea what the hell was going on. What was the point of running away? Why didn't you just tell me you were upset? What happened to being partners and working together? I thought we were getting somewhere, but apparently—"

"I know, okay?" I yell.

Hearing my own voice crack is the final straw. I suck in a shuddering breath and it spills out again as a loud sob. Tears start leaking down my cheeks as I hug myself tight, unable to meet Noah's eyes. I hate that I'm falling apart in front of him like this.

"I know I hurt you," I said. "I treated you like shit. You worked so hard to earn my friendship, my trust— and what did I do with yours? I was stupid and awful, and there's no excuse. But Brad just scared me so bad, I didn't know what to do. I—"

"Whoa, hey, wait a minute." Taken aback by my sudden breakdown, Noah sits down awkwardly beside me, his eyes wide. "Brad? What's he have to do with this? You didn't run away because of the inheritance contract?"

"What? No. Why would I?"

A look of disbelief and wonder crosses his handsome features. "Because I went to see you before the ceremony started and left it on your desk, right before you disappeared. What was I supposed to think?"

His confusion blurs things even more. I shake my head, trying to clear my thoughts enough to say what I need to. "That's not it. I need to tell you something."

I swallow hard to gather my courage. It's time to let down my defenses. Not only because Noah deserves an explanation, but because I've realized something. I trust him to help me without judging me. Like I should have trusted him all along.

"Right before the wedding started . . ."

Dammit, my voice won't stop trembling. I take a

deep breath. Maybe it'll help if I pretend I'm telling a story that happened to somebody else.

"Brad called me. He said he'd release . . . n-naked pictures of me if I didn't sell Tate & Cane to Daniels Media by next week. So that's why I left. I thought I could stop him, but then I realized I had no idea what to do. So I came back here to ask you for help."

There, I got through it. Not much detail, but I told the truth and the world didn't explode.

Although Noah just might. His nostrils flare and I watch in astonished horror as his face turns brick red. It would almost be funny if the situation weren't so dire.

Finally, very softly, Noah growls, "I'm going to rip his rotten dick off and feed it to him."

A hysterical little half giggle, half hiccup bursts from me. "Please don't."

I wipe my cheeks with the back of my hands, already feeling more in control. Noah's not going to let Brad win. More importantly, he's not going to let me go through this alone.

"Right. You probably already thought of that idea." Suddenly Noah's warm, strong arms enfold me tightly. He presses a gentle kiss to the crown of my head. "I wish you'd come to me sooner, Snowflake. You don't always have to bear everything alone."

And that fact seems so obvious now. I thought I understood that before, but now I've learned that Noah is here for me—for real, for always, no matter what.

Sniffling, I turn to wrap my arms around his waist and let myself relax into his comforting embrace. Our first hug that isn't motivated by a contract or a bet or anything but honest affection. It's pure and solid and exactly what I need. Already I'm starting to feel a little calmer.

"You've got me in your corner now," Noah murmurs into my hair. "I won't let anything happen to you."

My breathing slowly deepens and evens out as my tension ebbs away. I was so anxious about Brad's threat hanging over my head, but my fears seem much smaller with Noah here to help me fight them.

A few minutes later, he breaks the soothing silence to ask, "Do you want some tea?"

I give a weak chuckle through the last of my tears. "Wow, you really are English."

"Mum swore by it." Noah pulls back slightly, just enough to look at me. "And once you're feeling better, we can start figuring this thing out."

I nod. "Do you have any ideas?"

His lips curl up in a sly smile. "A few."

I grin back at Noah. Somehow I get the feeling that Brad is in deep shit. With Noah by my side, I feel safe for the first time since this disaster began.

Chapter Three

Noah

Olivia looks cute in the morning. She's still asleep, lying on her side, facing me, with the sheets tangled around her hips. Her tangled hair fans out behind her like spilled honey. Thank God she's not in that dreadful fleece onesie again. Her gauzy white tank top dips low to hint at the deep valley of her cleavage and rides up to expose the creamy soft expanse of her belly.

Forget cute, she looks positively edible. I want to run my tongue along the top of her breasts, tease her perky nipples through the thin fabric until she wakes up, moaning my name with her hands buried in my hair.

Not gonna happen, I know. This is Olivia we're talking about. Every victory is hard won, and every time I get close to her, she pulls back two steps further.

But a man can dream.

Eyes still closed, she stretches leisurely, letting out a little squeak as her long legs straighten under the bed linens. I appreciate the moment, admiring her as she wakes. My normal MO doesn't allow for sleepovers or morning-after encounters. But if this is what they're like, count me in.

After a moment, she blinks open her eyes.

"Hi," I say.

She swallows, her gaze dropping from mine as if she's self-conscious about me watching her wake up. "Hi."

"Are you ready for today?" After I calmed her frayed nerves, we spent hours last night going through my plan and rehearsing.

"You really think it will work?" she asks for the hundredth time.

But I understand why she's nervous. We're about to go toe-to-toe with one of the greatest bogeymen of her life.

Feeling a rush of protectiveness, I reply patiently, "I know it will." Men like Bradford Daniels are easy to outmaneuver. All they care about is their ego, and once you threaten that, they cave like little boys on the schoolyard.

I push the blankets off and sit up. There's coffee to make for Olivia, breakfast to prepare, and a hot shower calling my name.

"Holy m-morning wood," Olivia stutters, her eyes glued to the spot where my manhood is trying to escape my boxer briefs.

Down, boy.

I smirk at her. "What? He's happy to see you."

Her eyes lift to mine. "Really? You're glad I'm back?"

"Of course I am. What kind of question is that?" It's like she's constantly testing me, just waiting for me to slip up and tell her I'm done with her, with this game we're playing. To me, though, it's not just a game.

I want to tell her I've been awake for ten minutes, admiring the view, and this wood is exclusively for her. But I hold my tongue, sure that admission would freak her out.

"I just thought . . . when I left . . ." She pauses. "I was sure I ruined everything."

Having her back here in our bed makes me glad I didn't give in to all those baser instincts that told me to fuck and pillage my way through Manhattan when she left. I tip her chin up to force her to meet my eyes.

"You've got some making up to do, but nothing's ruined."

She nods, relief and gratitude shining in her eyes. And something else too—something so warm, something I don't dare to name, let alone hope for.

I hop out of bed and head toward the bathroom, wondering how all of this will unfold today, and in the days to follow.

• • •

Later, when we're dressed, fed, and ready, we stop in front of the building where Bradford Daniels works for his daddy's company. I can practically feel the apprehension flowing off Olivia in waves.

"Are you ready?" I ask.

She gives me a tight nod, her deep blue eyes full of worry. "No. But I don't think I'll ever be. We just have to go for it."

I squeeze her shoulder in reassurance. I'm almost . . . proud of her. She's shaking in her high heels and yet she's still standing here, ready to fight.

"We've got this," I promise her. "Don't look so worried."

It's time to grab the bull by the balls. I pull open the glass door, and we head inside and slip past the receptionist like we know where we're going. I figured that the element of surprise is always better when you're playing hardball.

But when we enter his corner office, Bradford looks like he was expecting us all along, with a smug grin stretched across his face.

"What, no pack of hungry lawyers? I figured that's where this was headed." Smirking like he's already won, Brad rises from his desk.

His office is furnished in a traditional style—a large free-standing mahogany desk facing the door, rows of bookshelves holding volumes of textbooks. A framed photograph of a rabbit hanging on the wall. *Okay, that last thing is weird . . .*

I stand my ground, gazing steadily at Brad, letting him know that his bullshit posturing doesn't intimidate me one bit. "We could come in here and threaten to sue your ass off, but we both know that would give you exactly the satisfaction you're looking for—a court battle, a media circus, Olivia's name dragged through the mud."

Brad's eyes narrow. "The mud? I think that's a bit optimistic. Olivia's name would mean *nothing* by the time I'm done with her."

Olivia shifts next to me. Her flinch is subtle, not enough for Brad to see, but I feel it. I reach over and take her hand.

"Anyway, we're not here to sue you," I continue. "We just thought we'd pay a visit to catch up. How's your old college buddy? What was his name . . . ?" I tap my lips, pretending to think. "Franklin Ashby?"

"How do you know him?" Brad responds just a

little too quickly. His eyes dart from mine to Olivia's, and his brow pinches unattractively.

Geez, what did she ever see in this pencil dick?

"Oh, come on," Olivia chimes in. "You two were roommates all through undergrad. Always bro-ing it up. Did you forget I was your girlfriend then?"

While we were strategizing last night, inspiration struck me when Olivia mentioned the name of Brad's college roommate. A name that I'd heard before, floating around New York's elite social circles. It only took a few quick phone calls to confirm everything.

But even though Olivia gave me this whole idea, the last thing we need right now is a verbal firefight between the two of them. I'm pretty sure that's what happened when he called her, and it got her nowhere. (Although it didn't exactly get Brad anywhere either.)

So I wave my hand in Olivia's direction to stop her. *Just let me do the talking for a little longer, baby.*

I start explaining to Brad exactly how screwed he is. "About six months ago, just before his company's big announcement, your friend Ashby exercised his stock options and purchased almost a quarter million shares. He made a killing." I rub my chin. "Funny, I seem to remember you doing pretty well too. Your stock trades even went through in the same week. Isn't that an interesting coincidence?"

"How do you know that?" Too late, Brad tries to recover. "I mean, what are you implying?"

"To answer your first question, Frank likes to brag when he's got a few drinks in him," I reply with a cheerful shrug. "And to your second question, insider trading."

The color drains from Brad's face. "You have no proof!"

I suppress a triumphant grin. "Maybe not right now. But the private investigator I hired to sift through the stock trade records for Frank's company and verify the personal connection between you two?" I suck my teeth with a loud *tsk*ing noise. "Within a few days, he'll have enough evidence for probable cause. And then you can explain to the SEC why you and Frank both purchased so many shares with such *convenient* timing."

That last part isn't strictly accurate. We haven't had time to hire a PI yet, although we can get one fast if we have to. But the truth doesn't matter. What matters is whether my bluff is convincing enough to get under Brad's skin. And judging by his reaction . . .

Brad's mouth opens and closes a few times.

Yeah, I'd say I've hit the nail on the head. I take the moment to enjoy the sight—the haughty heir of Daniels Media doing his best impression of a fish out of water.

"Th-this is a total crock of shit and you know it," he finally huffs out, placing a hand on his desk to lean in closer. "You both know I have you bent over, ready to take it, and this is how you're fighting back? Pathetic."

"You want to know what's pathetic?" I step closer to the asshat. Not because I particularly relish being near him, but because my six-foot-two-inch frame towers over his, what, five foot nine? It's bound to be intimidating. "The fact that Olivia here trusted you with pictures of her two gorgeous lemon-meringue pies and peach cobbler, and you, like the soulless weasel you are, tried to betray that trust in the worst possible way. Nothing gets me more livid than men who lack respect for women."

"Peach cobbler?" Brad asks.

When Olivia shoots me a strange look, I press on. "Yes, you know—her love box, her pink clam, her honey pot."

They're both looking at me with puzzled expressions.

I turn up my palms in exasperation. "Oh, for fuck's sake. Her pickle jar."

A giggle tumbles from Olivia's lips.

God, I love putting a smile on that woman's face.

Feigning a sudden realization, Olivia raises her finger, lips parting in pleasant surprise. "Oh, Noah! That reminds me of something."

"Yes, dear?" I ask, playing along.

"There's more."

"More? Do tell, Snowflake."

"I just remembered that one time, when Brad was

asleep, I snapped a picture of his little pickle."

Brad lets out a strangled noise.

Pretending not to notice—even though I'm struggling to keep a straight face—I raise my eyebrows at Olivia. "How little are we talking here?"

"Tiny. More like a miniature dill. A gherkin." She grins, knowing we're on a roll.

I let myself chuckle, the tense mood evaporating almost all at once. I have no idea if she's telling the truth, but we have this jackass right where we want him.

"No way! She doesn't have a picture of me," Brad stammers.

"Oh, but I do." She grins again. "It's such a teensy little thing, it almost slipped my memory."

I pat him on the back. "Tough luck, buddy, getting stuck with such a short straw. You're an eligible bachelor, right? You wouldn't want half of New York seeing that little dick of yours, would you?"

He purses his mouth. "No."

"Didn't think so." I pat him on the back again because, somehow, this meeting has turned into us saving the pompous Bradford Daniels from a public embarrassment so great, he'd never outrun it.

Olivia steps forward, her shoulders thrust back. "Then you will delete every copy, so help me God, on every device, anywhere that they exist."

Brad nods in agreement, looking defeated.

"And," I add, "you're going to sign this." I push a thin sheaf of papers across his desk. Olivia and I have already signed the last page.

"What the hell is it?" Brad grumbles wearily.

"A confession. Where we all agree, in writing, that you committed insider trading and attempted to extort Olivia into selling T&C . . . and in return for you not releasing her photos, we won't report any of your crimes. So if a single pic ever shows up online, consider this document your one-way ticket to federal prison." I give him a tight, humorless smile. "But as long as none of Olivia's nudes ever see the light of day, neither does your confession. What do you say?"

Brad swallows and his head bobs again. "Fine. Just get out."

He flips to the final page, scribbles his signature in a series of quick, angry slashes, and shoves it back into my hand.

Only once we're outside the ominous steel-and-glass building does Olivia give a little victory shout.

"You were incredible back there." Her eyes are alight with triumph, and her voice is almost giddy.

"You weren't so bad yourself," I reply with a grin. Counter-blackmail? I didn't know she had it in her.

"Seriously, did you see the look on his face when he thought the women of New York were going to find out about his teeny weenie? It was classic!" She giggles again.

"Do you really have a photo of it?"

She shakes her head with a chuckle. "Nope. I was totally bluffing." In a stage whisper she adds, "It wasn't photo worthy."

I laugh out loud. Brilliant—that's just icing on the

cake. I want to tease her by saying *I'm so proud*. But that feels weird for some reason, so I settle for, "Remind me never to play poker with you."

Buoyant with victory, we stroll along the sidewalk back toward the car.

"Noah?" she asks after a few minutes.

"Yeah, Snowflake?"

"Thank you for helping me. And for not judging me for sending those photos in the first place."

"Hey, the only thing I cared about was putting that asshole in his place. I'd never judge a woman for sexting her boyfriend."

"Still, you dropped everything to help me. After I just . . . ran."

The urge to reach out, to lace our fingers together or put my hand on her waist or just touch her in some small way, flares up inside me. But I don't. Not yet. With all the commotion Brad's blackmailing caused, I still don't quite know where Olivia and I stand. She did run out on our wedding instead of including me in her personal drama. And she still hasn't said a peep about the contract. Even if this victory is pretty fucking incredible, I'm not ready to celebrate yet. I need answers.

"Should we head back to the office?" Olivia checks her phone, and the time shows just after eleven.

"Not yet. Let's go get lunch."

"Good idea."

Thirty minutes later, we're seated at a Mediterranean restaurant that's just around the corner from our office, sipping iced tea and munching on hummus and warm pita bread.

"God, the look on his face . . ." Olivia chuckles again. "I won't forget that anytime soon. Thank you for today. For everything."

I nod. "It was nothing." *Just connecting a few dots.*

"And for what it's worth, I am so sorry about leaving you high and dry at the beach."

I tense my jaw. Do I wish she would have trusted me with this information and let me help from the start?

Sure. But I've never been in Olivia's shoes, and I can't judge her decision. I have no idea how I'd feel if my ex was threatening to expose me—literally—if I didn't cut her into my company. Shit, I'm almost as hard-headed as Olivia; I probably would have wanted to handle it alone too. But there's still something bugging me.

"About that . . . is the blackmail the only reason you ran away?"

Her eyes lift to mine. "Of course. I told you I was ready to tie the knot, and I meant that."

I nod. I almost ask her how she feels about marrying *me*, specifically. But at the last second, I decide I'm not ready to hear the answer to that loaded question. I need to remember that we're both doing this out of necessity.

I have responsibilities, mountains of obligations. The fear of failure is reason enough to stay the course.

Chapter Four

Olivia

I expected to be nervous again. And I am, but just a little—not nearly so bad as before. Even though my palms are sweating like crazy, my heart beats steady and my stomach is calm. I almost feel like I'm floating as Noah and I stand once again before the justice of the peace.

She recites our wedding vows over the hushed lapping of the ocean waves, the mewing cries of seagulls, the occasional clang of buoys and ship's bells. Our two rows of guests watch from their folding chairs on the beach. And the whole thing just feels *right* in a way it didn't before. As if some invisible puzzle piece has clicked into place. My doubts have finally worn themselves away, leaving me light and free.

The judge presents our marriage license and the inheritance contract, all filled out except for the final signature line. Noah signs first, then me, my pen gliding over the paper as easily as the distant sailboats glide through the water. Finally, after all our false starts, our two signatures sit side by side.

"You may now kiss the bride," says the judge with a smile.

The guests applaud and laugh as Noah pulls me close. I grin against his mouth, a warm light blooming in my chest. It suddenly strikes me that Noah has always been there for me. And not just lately, like with Brad—when we were growing up too. He's been a constant in my life ever since we were toddlers. Playful, sometimes irritating, always magnetic, never far out of reach.

Noah has done so much for my sake, especially in the past month. He's gone so far out of his way. The thought of how deeply he must care about me is both giddy and humbling. I'm still not sure about the romance and sex parts of being married, but our friendship is beyond doubt. We're a team. Ready to face whatever the future holds.

But as right as it feels to be here with Noah, the fact of our marriage is still staggering. *Holy shit, I'm a wife now.* I need some quiet time alone to let this sink in.

When the informal reception is over and everyone starts throwing away their paper plates and gathering their purses and jackets for the trip back to the city, I breathe a sigh of relief. I say good-bye to Dad, Camryn, and the rest of the guests, then retreat to the quiet of my family's summer cottage.

Grabbing my laptop bag, I head to my old bedroom. Its desk is more than a little cramped now that I'm an adult. But this house is too small for a separate study, and I'd rather be in my own space than the master bedroom right now. I don't want to give Noah any funny ideas about sharing a bed on our wedding night.

I push up the window to let in the ocean breeze, fold myself into my undersized desk chair, and open my laptop, ready to immerse myself in work.

But my peaceful solitude doesn't last long. Footsteps approach from down the hall and stop on my threshold.

"What are you doing here?" Noah's voice asks behind me.

Glancing out of the corner of my eye, I reply flatly, "This is my room."

Noah points at my laptop like it's an angry rattlesnake. "No, I mean what are you doing with that thing?"

"Strategic analysis." As should be obvious from my spreadsheet-covered screen.

He frowns. "Right now? After we just got married?"

"What else would I do?" My tone has cooled, daring him to contradict me. I know damn well what's on his mind, but there's no way I'm even putting that suggestion on the table. He's a big boy—he can use his own words. Not that begging will get him anywhere.

Noah comes inside to sit on the bed, facing me. "I know you're a workaholic, Snowflake, but this is ridiculous. We can afford to take our wedding night off."

"Can we? After all the time and money I've wasted . . ."

I bite my lip, still ashamed of what happened on our first attempt at a wedding. And while seeing Brad cut down to size was insanely satisfying, the attorney who drafted that agreement wasn't cheap. Tate & Cane's pockets are a lot shallower than they used to be.

Noah reaches out to gently cup my chin. "Hey. You didn't waste anything—you didn't cause any of this. It was that asshole who decided to mess with you. And we had to stop him, because nobody hurts my girl and gets away with it." He raises his eyebrows at me for emphasis. "So don't you dare blame yourself."

Taken aback, I can't help a small smile. *He always defends me . . . even against myself.* Noah's earnest words mean so much. Almost too much.

"Okay, fair enough. I'll try to lay off the self-hate. Still, we have to get back on schedule."

"We should at least spend tonight together," he insists.

I roll my eyes, still smiling. "Jesus, you're relentless. Fine. Then I hope you brought your laptop too, because this business plan isn't going to write itself."

"I'm afraid not," he says, raising his eyebrows, "since I *assumed* we'd be on vacation. I'll just have to read over your shoulder."

He leaves and brings back a wooden chair from the kitchen, pushes it next to mine, and sits down. Close enough for me to feel his body's distracting warmth.

He occasionally reaches out and touches me—little brushes against my wrist, his hand at the small of my back, making me hyper-aware of him and his distinct maleness. My heart riots with each movement.

This is what I've been trying to avoid all along— the seeds of hope blooming in my chest. I need to stamp those feelings out now because I know what Noah's doing. He's putting on a brace front and trying to make the best of our situation. It's only a matter of time before this whole charade comes crashing down around us, leaving my heart in tatters.

My real happily-ever-after is out there, somewhere. And when we right the proverbial ship that is Tate & Cane Enterprises, I'll be able to think about things like getting our marriage annulled and moving on, but until then, it's heads down.

"So, what are your thoughts so far?" Noah asks in a low tone that sounds way too intimate for staring at a bunch of financial graphs.

Trying to ignore his intense gaze, I start explaining my arguments for how we should structure our plan of attack.

We collaborate late into the night. At some point, a bottle of champagne appears on the desk at my elbow. I don't know how—I was too absorbed in work to notice Noah moving. All I know is that when I turn my head, I see a foil-topped green bottle and two glasses that weren't there before.

Immediately I say, "I'm not going to get drunk with you." I can't afford to let my guard down, only to find my clothes strewn across the bedroom floor come morning and a delicious ache present between my thighs. Even if I might want to. *No, Olivia.* I silently scold myself. *Bad pussy.*

"Who said anything about getting drunk?" Noah replies breezily. "I just thought it might be nice to have a drink while we work. Sure, we're both very busy people, but we still just got married. Let's celebrate the imminent revival of Tate & Cane."

The idea is surprisingly tempting. I make a thoughtful noise . . . then give in. "Fair enough. But just one drink." Maybe a little bubbly buzz will help me be more creative. Plus this man is just damn hard to say no to.

Noah pours the two flutes full, then raises his with a deliberately overdramatic flourish. "To Tate & Cane Enterprises, may you rise again. And to Snowflake, my brilliant, drop-dead gorgeous wife who's going to pull our asses out of the red."

My cheeks flush a little. I clink my glass against his, trying to hide my smile. "I thought this toast was going to be about business."

He chuckles. "But you're so cute when you're flattered, Snowflake."

"Don't give yourself so much credit," I mutter. But he's totally right. He does get me flustered easily. I take my first sip of champagne, then add, "Thanks, Noah."

He looks up with a devilish grin. "It's our wedding night. Not even a kiss? What happened to first base?"

The tip of his tongue traces slowly over his full lips, bringing mental images that are a lot more explicit than just kissing.

Dammit, I'm staring at his mouth. "S-stop screwing around and help me work," I snap.

• • •

Early the next morning, I wake up in my desk chair with a nagging headache and keyboard prints on my cheek. I sit up with a pained groan—my spine did *not* like being hunched over my desk for six hours. I can practically hear it creak.

Something soft and heavy slides off my back. I look around, confused, and see a blanket pooled on the floor behind me. I definitely didn't do that. If I was lucid enough to get a blanket last night, I would have been aware enough to stop working and get to bed before I fell asleep. Noah must have covered me up.

And where is he, anyway?

Rubbing the sleep out of my eyes, I stand and look around. I'm disappointed to see no sign of him. I guess he slept in the master bedroom after it became clear that

I wouldn't be touching his dick.

Well, that's a good thing, isn't it? I can speed through my morning routine without any interruptions and get to the airport with plenty of time.

When I arrive downstairs in the kitchen, Noah is at the stove, frying up half a dozen eggs over easy. I have a flash of déjà vu back to our first morning in our new penthouse apartment. Although he's wearing a shirt this time . . . too bad. He wears the bed-head look well.

Who am I kidding? The sexy jerk wears everything well.

"Have a nice wedding night?" he asks without turning around, sounding amused. Teasing me yet again.

I guess this is what I have to look forward to for the rest of my life. I comment breezily, "Well, there was this one asshole who kept hanging around while I was trying to work . . ."

"Sounds like a problem. Maybe I should have a word with him after we eat."

I walk over and stop behind him. I hesitate, then loop my arms around his firm waist, resting my cheek on the base of his neck. His movements pause for a second; he obviously wasn't expecting that.

"Hey," I murmur. "I wanted to thank you again. For helping me handle Brad." As much as I hate to admit it, I don't know what I would have done without Noah. "And for . . . I don't know. Everything. Putting up with all my shit." I tend to get a little bat-shit crazy when it comes to work.

His chuckle rumbles through his back and into my chest. "Don't be silly, Snowflake. What else are husbands for?"

Gratitude washes through me. I breathe deeply, inhaling his clean, faintly spicy scent, and sigh it out into his hair. That was so easy. Everything about being with Noah is so much easier than I ever thought a relationship could be. Although I admit I don't have the best examples to work from. Noah has seen me at my worst and yet he's still here, cooking me breakfast, letting me hold him. Forgiving me like it's nothing.

For a moment, I just indulge in this atmosphere of warm, calm security. Then I reluctantly peel myself off my new husband's back and start preparing our coffee and tea.

We take our breakfast outside to eat on the front porch while watching the sailboats bobbing in the harbor. I meant to enjoy the view, but only about ten minutes pass before we're deep in shop talk. Noah floats several new ideas for our proposal that I wish I'd thought of. I make a mental note to add them to our draft while we're in the air.

In the air. Wait a minute. I squint through the window to check the kitchen's wall clock—and then I jump up from the patio table.

"Shit, we're going to miss our plane!"

Noah shrugs, taking another leisurely sip of his tea. "No big deal. We can always catch the next one."

My withering look says it all.

"All right, all right." He holds up his hands in surrender. "Back to the grindstone."

• • •

We arrive back at the Tate & Cane building after lunchtime. My empty stomach feels tight as I walk down its halls. I'm almost certainly being paranoid, but it feels like I'm doing a walk of shame. Like everyone knows that last night was my wedding night. It doesn't matter that I didn't even fuck Noah—everyone must assume I did, right?

Jeez . . . maybe I should have. If I was going to endure an awkward morning after, I might as well have enjoyed a fun night beforehand.

Wait, hell no. Don't even entertain the thought of fucking Noah. That way lies madness. Even though he clearly wants me and part of me wants him back, because his damn sexy face and voice and body and wicked words always hit me right in the . . .

Cheeks burning, I hurry to my office. I e-mail Dad the draft of our proposal, pour myself a giant cup of coffee, and check my backlog of messages. The tedious task works almost as well as a cold shower.

Half an hour later, I get a reply from Dad.

Proposal looks great. Let's discuss? I'll order in pastramis from Sal's.

I smile to myself. Dad knows that place is my favorite deli. And evidently, he also knows that I haven't eaten since before our flight. I close my laptop and walk to his office.

As I open his door, Dad beams at me from behind his desk. "Your work is top-notch as always. When did you even find the time to write this?"

"Noah and I worked together last night." As much of a nuisance as Noah made himself, he deserves due credit.

Dad's expression morphs from pride into pity. "Last night? Oh, sweetie—"

"It's fine," I say, interrupting him. I don't want to hear two different men protest about my wedding night in less than twenty-four hours. And even though my sex life is nonexistent, discussing it with my own father would still be just way too gross. "So, what were your thoughts on the proposal?"

Dad sighs, but takes the hint. "It looks better than anything I've come up with. I guess I made the right decision, putting you kids on the case."

Something in his tone makes me narrow my eyes. "I sense a 'but' coming."

"I'm not sure where we're going to get the money for all this training."

"What do you mean? I double-checked our budget. Unless . . ." I trail off, worrying my lip. "Did something happen while I was gone?"

He nods grimly. "Red Dog Optics pulled out. Halfway through a project. They're paying us for the deliverables we finished, plus our early termination fee, but everything we had in progress . . . labor down the drain. And of course, we can't count on that future income anymore."

I pinch the bridge of my nose hard, trying to ward off an impending stress headache. That's one of our biggest clients—well, it *was*, anyway. *Son of a bitch*. I'm out of the office for less than two full workdays, and look what I miss.

Thank God I didn't let Noah persuade me to catch a later flight.

"Why the hell would they do that?" I ask. "We've lost clients before . . ." By which I mean, we've been steadily bleeding them for years now. "But never so suddenly. Why not ride out our current contract and then just avoid signing another one?"

Dad shakes his head. "No idea. Our work on that project seemed up to our usual standard, as far as I could tell. The only explanation I can think of is that something spooked them."

"What, they thought we'd collapse before we could even finish their project?" I lick my raw lip nervously.

Tate & Cane certainly isn't doing great, and I knew our reputation would take a hit after the board started meeting with buyers and word got around . . . but our situation isn't nearly bad enough to make Red Dog react like this.

I take a deep breath, forcing myself to calm down. I'm being paranoid. Some dumbass probably just made a careless comment to his golf buddy, it got misinterpreted, and the rumor mill spun out of control. If anything suspicious happens again, then maybe we should investigate. But for now, we don't have the time or resources to spend on a wild goose chase.

"Then we'll just have to find a consultant who's willing to handle our training for cheap," I say with a lot more confidence than I feel. *Hopefully we won't get what we pay for.* "And we can concentrate on winning back some old clients before we try to court new ones."

"Sounds like a plan, sweetie. I'm behind you kids all the way." Dad leans forward on his desk. "I'm counting on you to get creative and save this thing we've built together . . . not just for the sake of your futures, but for your children too."

I give him a confused look. "Children? That's a pretty long ways off, Dad." Reproducing isn't on my radar at all. I haven't wanted babies since I learned they weren't really brought by storks.

Dad gives my confused look right back. "Not that far off . . . ?"

My phone chimes. I pull it out and see a text.

NOAH: You hear about Red Dog?

"Sorry, Dad." I sigh, not very sorry at all to get off the topic of children. *Thanks for the conversational escape hatch, Noah.* "I should probably go meet with Noah to get started on this. Can you tell the delivery guy to take my pastrami to my office when he gets here?"

Dad nods good-bye and I hustle to Noah's office, far away from any ten-pound hints about starting a family. That last part of our chat was surreal. I'm sure Dad has a whole fairy-tale ending envisioned for Noah and me, but seriously? I'm not even close to the motherly type.

Okay, back into work mode. We have to figure out how to start implementing our business plan on the cheap and recovering at least a few old clients. Noah can definitely help on both of those fronts. Persuasion is his specialty . . . sweet-talking, haggling deals, calling in favors. And if there's a woman in any position of influence, he can turn on the playboy charm and use his handsome face to help sway her. Like he did with Estelle Osbourne at Clair de Lune.

I set my jaw as I walk a little faster. Remembering

that dinner still pisses me off way more than it should. It's not like Noah is really my husband. Hell, I never wanted him to be "mine" at all, in any sense of the word.

At least, I didn't want that a month ago. Maybe even two weeks ago. But now, maybe ... I think I might. God, I don't even know. My feelings have gotten so complicated lately. I think of Noah's mischievous smile, his low, smooth voice saying my name ...

Then I push those thoughts right out of my head. We are professionals. *I'm* a professional. Our job is to get our company through this quagmire. That one single problem is what we'll eat, sleep, and breathe until we convince the board to reverse their decision about selling Tate & Cane. We have no room for emotions or desires.

Maybe Noah is right about me being an ice queen sometimes. But right now, with over six thousand futures hanging in the balance, that's so much safer than being human. I just need to maintain my focus and composure, and pray that we'll get through this.

Chapter Five

Noah

When Sterling texted me asking how the wedding night went, rather than answer, I asked him to meet me for lunch.

My best friend has a way with the fairer sex, and I'm hopeful he has some advice for me about how to proceed after my less-than-stellar wedding night. It wasn't that I expected Olivia to drop to her knees and service me, or spread her legs in our marital bed, but a good-night kiss would have been nice. *Sheesh.*

"That bad, eh?" Sterling asks when I slide into the chair across from him.

"The wedding night? A fucking disaster."

He doesn't have to reply because his eyes say it all. In those honey-colored depths fringed in dark lashes that women go nuts over—*the lucky bastard*—is a mixture of pity and curiosity. But he says, "Tell your good mate all about it," leaning back in his seat with his fingers laced behind his head.

Thankfully I'm saved from his Dr. Phil-style self-help entertainment with the approach of our waitress.

"What can I get you gentlemen?" she asks.

When I asked Sterling to lunch, he agreed on the condition that we go to his favorite British-style pub. Despite having English blood pumping through my veins, I despise the food. Sterling was born and raised in the countryside outside of London. He still has a taste for it—reminds him of his youth, I guess.

He places an order for the ploughman's lunch, and I choose the least noxious thing I can find on the menu—fish and chips. Tea is the one thing we can agree on.

When the waitress saunters away, he's back to smirking at me expectantly. "So, do tell. How's the wifey?"

If he bats those fucking eyelashes at me one more time, like we're having girl talk, I'm going to slug the son of a bitch.

"At least let me get my tea before you badger me," I mutter.

The waitress delivers a little porcelain kettle with piping-hot brew. It reminds me of the one I have at home. I think of Olivia and something inside me pinches. She tapped away on her keyboard until late last night; whether she was determined to get her thoughts on paper or to keep her distance from me, I wasn't sure.

"I'm not trying to badger you," Sterling says with a sigh. "Just wondering what's the problem. I take it the wedding night wasn't all you dreamed it might be?"

"You could say that." I take a sip of my tea and find it's the perfect temperature.

"Is she still as icy as ever, or is she warming to you?"

"We spent all night going over a new business plan," I say.

"Christ on a cracker. The woman is a ballbuster."

"Tell me about it."

It's true that Olivia is relentless in her pursuit of

perfection. She's smart and determined, and she never wavers in confidence. It's sexy as hell. Frustrating. But admirable.

Nothing fazes the woman. She's smart as a whip, and doesn't take shit from anyone. I've never once seen her back down from a challenge. What I *have* seen is her effortlessly dominating executive meetings filled with industry veterans—men old enough to be her grandfather, who were in business suits before she was out of diapers. And she doesn't even notice or care how beautiful she is . . .

I realize Sterling is still watching me and snap out of my thoughts. They were getting too gooey for my own good, anyway.

"She sure as hell doesn't act like anybody's wife," I mutter.

He shrugs. "So she isn't a romantic."

Actually, according to her friend Camryn, she is. But I don't tell that to Sterling at the risk of sounding like a total cliché.

"She fell asleep at her desk sometime after

midnight."

"You don't become that successful at the age of twenty-six by taking your eye off the ball."

"I guess."

"So I can assume that baby-making isn't going well?" He chuckles.

"Not exactly."

"What are you going to do? A woman's never refused you before, and now your own wife won't fuck you." He makes a disappointed noise in his throat.

When I merely flip him off, he excuses himself for a visit to the restroom. When Sterling is gone, I pull out my phone and check my messages.

There are three e-mails from Fred, all of them about the dire situation of the company, and another from Preston informing me that the board is having an "exploratory meeting" with a rival firm next week.

Fuck.

I close out my in-box. Since Sterling still isn't back,

I pull up the business news app on my phone to scroll through the headlines, hoping to take my mind off all the bed news at work.

"Can Manhattan's New "Power Couple" Turn a Marketing Dinosaur Around Before It's Too Late?"

I begin reading the top article, only to discover that it's about Olivia and me. Financial advisors are speculating about the future of the company and predict a plummet in our stock price as leadership changes are shaken out.

Well, fuck that. I won't watch our company go down in flames. But the truth is, we're not even close to being out of the woods yet. And all this bad press is bound to hobble us even more.

Frustrated, I slam my phone down on the table just as Sterling approaches.

"What now?" he asks, sliding into his seat and laying his napkin across his lap.

It feels like my work life and personal life are both imploding. I'm not used to failing so miserably. Feeling so helpless.

Then I realize something—the solution to both my problems is winning over Olivia. We have to work together to save this shipwreck, and I'm tired of her rejections, her pessimistic idea that we can never work. *Fuck that.*

"I know what I need to do," I blurt.

"And what's that?"

"I need to seduce my wife. I need to show her how good we can be together."

Sterling nods. "So, what are you going to do? Plan some big elaborate date to woo her?"

I think it over, then shake my head. "No. Olivia's much too skittish. It'll take more finesse than that."

• • •

When Olivia arrives home from the gym at seven, I'm ready. I turned down the lighting in the penthouse and put on some smooth jazz to play softly in the background.

She sets her gym bag on the floor, giving me a skeptical look. "What's going on?"

She's probably reading the mood as a romantic one, and I'm not sure if that's good or bad. My goal is just to get her to relax tonight.

Trying to act natural, I reply, "I got some dinner for us and thought we could take the night off from spreadsheets and numbers."

She shrugs. "Sure. Let me grab a quick shower, then I'll be right out."

I expected more of a fight. Maybe the gods are looking down on me tonight with pity.

Toeing off her hot pink tennis shoes, Olivia heads toward the bathroom. When I hear the spray of the shower, I head into the kitchen to finalize everything.

The food arrives by the time I hear the shower shut off. I arrange the contents of the takeout containers on a couple of small plates, to keep with the tapas theme.

There's goat cheese with roasted figs, seared scallops, and a potato-and-gruyere gratin. It smells great. I pour two glasses of cabernet sauvignon and carry everything to the coffee table in the living room.

I hear Olivia's footsteps on the wood floor and look up. Fresh out of the shower, she's dressed in a pair of black leggings that hug every last curve of her shapely legs and round ass, along with a gray sweatshirt that's cut to hang off one bare shoulder, exposing her lightly freckled skin. She looks dewy and flushed from the shower, and I want to touch her to see if she feels as warm and soft as she looks.

"Wow. What's all this?" she asks, sitting down beside me on the couch.

"Just a casual dinner. I thought we deserved some relaxation, considering the pressure we're under at work."

She accepts the glass of wine I hand her, and takes a sip. "How thoughtful."

The sweet scent of her honeysuckle-and-vanilla body wash hits me square in the face, making me want to lean in and taste her skin, her lips, her breasts.

Shit.

I need to get it together. My plan is to win her over, to woo her, not to push myself on her with unwanted advances.

She may have a tough exterior, but I'm starting to learn that she's actually a little timid when it comes to getting physical with me. Which is not at all what I'm used to. Most other women would love a ride on Noah Tate.

Olivia helps herself to a portion of each dish—cutting off a little bite of sea scallop, letting out a little murmur of pleasure as she chews, blowing on a steaming forkful of potato gratin before closing her lips around it.

"So good," she says with a moan. "How did you know I love tapas?"

I shrug. "I may have pumped Camryn for information."

Her eyes flick over to mine as she takes another sip of wine. "Why would you do that?"

Returning her gaze, I decide to make myself vulnerable. "Because I like you, Olivia. I want this to work."

And I don't just mean that in the sense of taking back our company and making a fuck-ton of money. I genuinely think that if she is willing to try, we can have a shot at being a real, happy couple. But I don't clarify all that extra stuff. Olivia appreciates honesty, but there's such a thing as baring too much too soon. Or possibly at all.

I already know we're compatible when it comes to the major stuff—politics, religion, and work ethic—but I'm starting to think that together in the bedroom, we'd be explosive. She tries to deny it, but the way her body responds to me is ridiculous. Not to mention the desperate way I crave her luscious ass and her perky tits, even her smart mouth is ridiculous. I'm normally a hit-it-and-quit-it type of guy. Once I've had a taste, I'm done and on to the next course. But something tells me that with Olivia, once wouldn't be nearly enough.

First, though, I need to know how she's feeling about all of this. With the threat of Brad's blackmail looming over us, demanding all our attention, I've barely gotten a chance to talk to her about the wedding, the contract, and especially the baby-making that needs to happen. We need to discuss this elephant in the room like mature, responsible adults.

"So, how do you feel about kids?" I ask.

Her eyebrows shoot up. "Kids?"

I nod slowly, now confused as well as nervous. Why is she so shocked?

"I, um . . . well, I guess I haven't really thought about them," she stammers.

My stomach grows uneasy. How in the fuck has she not thought about it? This is Olivia, the woman who weighs every decision with a list of pros and cons. Her childhood letters to Santa were probably formatted in official memo style with bulleted requests.

"Why? You're not thinking about . . ." She's so flustered that she leaves the rest of her sentence unfinished.

Of fucking course I'm thinking about it. We have a contractual obligation to fulfill. Period.

Then realization slams into me all at once.

Holy. Fuck.

"On the day of our wedding, did you read the contract or did you just sign it?" I ask, trying to keep my tone neutral.

She shrugs, curling her legs under her on the couch. "Signed it. I already knew what it said. Dad and Prescott must have explained everything a hundred times at all those meetings we had."

I never expected Olivia of all people to sign a contract without reading it. I'm so stunned that I just stay quiet as the minutes tick past and we continue sipping our wine.

I try to calm down and think through this. But I'm stumped. The contract is finalized now—we're legally bound. We've *been* legally bound for almost a week at this point. And now that I've been quiet about it for so long . . . how do I tell her without making it seem like I was lying all along?

Plus, I'm ninety-nine percent sure she'll rip up the contract and storm off, and the deal will fall apart. I can't let that happen. No inheritance means no second chance from the board. Which, in turn, means that everyone at Tate & Cane—innocent people like Rosita, who depend on the jobs we provide—will be royally fucked.

I can't let anything happen to jeopardize this deal. I can't afford to take even the smallest risk. I'll just have to win Olivia over with my charm and let it all happen naturally. Well, as natural as impregnating your fake wife can be.

Besides, even if I told her about the heir clause and she miraculously didn't go nuclear, that would just put pressure on her to get pregnant for our company's sake. Having a kid wouldn't be a free choice. It's better if I pitch her the idea on its own merits.

I'm up to the task, right? I've already done something similar; she used to hate my guts, and it took me less than a month to woo her into marrying me. Changing her mind about kids will be a lot tougher, but I just have to take things up another notch. Really put my back into it. Be my most charming, appealing self. If anyone can make a woman fall in love, deep enough to start a family . . .

But Olivia isn't just any woman. I suppress a despairing groan. Fuck me sideways . . . I've got my work cut out for me.

What in the hell do I do now?

"So, what else is on the agenda, Mr. Tate?"

Olivia smiles warmly at me like she has no idea about the inner war I'm waging. I've refilled her wineglass twice, and something tells me she's feeling tipsy and carefree.

That makes one of us.

I stack the empty plates, carry them into the kitchen, and pile them in the sink. Then I just stand there, my hands gripping the edge of the countertop. I need a minute. I feel like the apartment is closing in on me.

Before I make any big decisions about how to approach this problem, I need to think carefully. But with my head spinning and Olivia waiting expectantly in the other room, I can't do that here. I have to take things one step at a time.

So the question is: what the hell do I do right now?

"Noah? Are you coming back?" she calls.

I take a deep breath and return to her side. Realizing I can't let this unpleasant surprise distract me from my plan, I decide to push forward. Tonight was supposed to be about getting her to relax, unwind, and trust me. There's no point in ruining the whole evening by thoughtlessly blurting out everything. I'll figure out a graceful way to tell her later.

"You've been so wound up from work. We both have," I say as I sit back down.

She nods, agreeing.

"Tonight I was hoping we could set all that aside and chill together."

She smiles at me. "Very good idea. I don't chill nearly enough."

Part of me is almost shocked that she's going along with this so easily. The rest of me is still busy reeling from the realization that she has no idea I'm supposed to get her pregnant within the next three months. Actually, it's more like two months now.

Olivia sets her wineglass on the table and rolls her shoulders, sighing softly.

"What's wrong?" I ask.

"Just a little tight, is all."

I inhale through my nose. I have to shove the pregnancy stuff to the back corner of my brain. We're a long way off from Olivia letting me pump her full of my semen anyhow, so why am I stressing about it now? The first step is showing her how compatible we can be.

And that starts now.

I smile at her. "Sit tight. I'll be right back."

I grab a bottle of massage oil from the hall closet and return to the living room. The soft jazz music seems to float in the air, creating a pleasant buzz in the atmosphere.

Olivia's eyes widen when I rejoin her on the couch, but she doesn't question me.

"I'll give you a massage," I suggest. "Take off your sweatshirt."

Olivia flinches, chewing on her lip while she watches me. "But I'm not wearing anything underneath."

That's the idea. "I promise not to look."

She hesitates for another second, then turns her back to me and pulls her shirt over her head, dropping it to the floor. The creamy canvas in front of me is one to be admired. The twin dimples in her lower back near the band of her leggings would make lesser men weep.

I warm a few drops of oil between my palms and rest my hands on her stiff shoulders.

"Relax. Okay?"

She gives me a swift nod.

I work my fingers into the knots I can feel under her skin, and when I press my thumbs in next to her spine, she moans.

"Dear God, that feels good."

"Been a while?" I ask, just a hint of mischief in my voice.

"Since I had a massage? Yeah."

I meant to ask if it had been a while since she enjoyed a man's touch, but at the last second, I decide not to clarify my question. The last thing I want to hear about is my wife's past conquests. No fucking thank you.

I continue caressing her tense muscles and feel her slowly begin to relax. Knowing her breasts are bare and just out of my reach is practically a cardinal sin. Trying to figure out a way to entice Olivia for more, I say, "If you turn around, I can reach the front of your shoulders better."

Total lie. I'm hoping she can't read my mind.

When she hesitates for a few seconds, I lean in and kiss the back of her neck. "You're my wife, sweetheart. It's no big deal."

Those words hang between us, blossoming into something more than I think either of us ever dreamed.

She swallows, then slowly begins to turn toward me.

Catching her lower lip between her teeth, her eyes glossy with desire, Olivia faces me on the couch.

Without saying a word, I drizzle a few more drops

of oil into my palms before rubbing them together. I massage the front of her shoulders, her upper arms, and fight off the erection pressing against my zipper.

Olivia's breathing has changed—the entire mood surrounding us has changed. My gaze dips down briefly, and I watch as her nipples harden into little pebbled knots.

Unable to resist the temptation she's placed before me, I cup the weight of her breasts in my palms and rub my thumbs across her nipples.

Olivia draws a shuddering breath, her lips parting in surprise.

My fingers, slick from the fragrant oil, glide easily over her skin as I rub her nipples in small, circular movements.

A tiny groan—just barely audible—slips past her lips, and I dive in for a kiss, knowing she's silently aching for more. My tongue pushes past her lips and she kisses me back, hard and passionate. I've got her right where I want her. Wet. And ready for me.

As we kiss, I move my body over hers until she's

lying on the couch and I'm balanced over her. Her thighs part, inviting me even closer, and I nestle in until my steely shaft finds her warm center. Olivia gasps, breaking apart from the kiss. The contact is deliciously frustrating—so close and yet so far, separated only by a few layers of clothes. But if I have my way, they'll be gone soon enough. My mouth moves to her neck as I continue circling my hips, bumping against her clit with each movement.

"Is this okay?" I murmur and wait in agony as she pauses, her eyes searching mine.

"Don't stop," she breathes, her hips lifting to find that friction once again.

I lean down and take one ripe nipple in my mouth, rolling my tongue over it and sucking on the firm tip.

Olivia cries out in pleasure. "Noah . . ."

My name on her lips, in that sweet, gravelly voice laden with desire, snaps the last thread of my restraint. I kneel and grab the sides of her yoga pants, peeling them and her panties down her legs until she's bare to me.

Christ. My cock surges, leaking pre-cum in my

boxers. Olivia's body is perfection. Soft milky curves, full breasts, and a bare pussy with a pink clit peeking at me from between her juicy lips. I want to wrap my lips around it and suck until she screams. I won't—not yet, anyway, but I can't help reaching down to touch her. Running a fingertip down the length of her cleft, I stroke the soft, swollen bud lightly. Olivia lets out a tiny, pleading whimper.

I'm trying to go slow, I swear I am, but with Olivia naked and writhing on the couch, looking up at me with those huge blue eyes of hers, it's nearly impossible. Fighting with myself to slow down and remember my manners, I stroke her clit with one careful fingertip, while my other hand caresses her breasts, thumbing her nipples.

Is there a polite way to say, *Ride my face until you come all over my tongue?*

"Everything okay, princess?" I ask instead, my voice husky with desire.

"It feels so good."

She watches my hand as I continue my slow,

torturous movements, lightly rubbing her clit, wanting to draw out her pleasure. I can feel how wet she is for me, and use the moisture to sweep across her swollen bud, back and forth, back and forth.

A whimper of frustration rises up her throat, and I know I have her right where I want her. There's no way she's walking away from this—from us—until I've given her what she needs.

Olivia's thighs open wider as she brings her heels up toward her butt. My view is fucking perfect. I can watch every shuddering breath that racks her chest, every heartbeat that makes her pulse riot in her throat, and every tiny quiver as I tease her pussy with light touches.

"You're beautiful like this," I say. "So responsive and wet."

She moans again, circling her hips to meet my touch. "Noah . . . it's been so long . . ."

When I think she can't take any more of my teasing, I slide off the couch so I'm kneeling on the floor. Then I tug her hips until her ass rests on the edge of the sofa and her knees are spread wide enough to accommodate my shoulders.

"I'm going to make you come with my mouth. If you don't want that, you better tell me now."

We're so close that I know she can feel my hot breath between her legs. She nods, her breasts heaving with anticipation.

Then I seal my lips around her swollen clit and suck—hard.

Her hips jerk up, her body trembling at my onslaught of erotic kisses. I have to hold her in place, clamping both hands around her thighs to keep her spread for me.

"Come on, baby, let go," I whisper against her slick flesh, and then continue devouring her.

She's breathing hard and whimpering softly, her moans so fucking sexy. Her taste, her scent, her cries of pleasure are all so intoxicating. It unleashes something inside me.

I can do this all night . . . but soon her entire body

goes as rigid as an arrow and her hands push into my hair.

I lick her, over and over, smiling when she cries out.

"Oh God, yes!"

In a frenzy I lick her, my rhythm too fast, but I couldn't slow myself down right now if I wanted to. She's so close, and I want to be the one to take her there.

Olivia shouts my name as tremors ripple through her whole body. Just as she starts to come, I push one finger inside her, unable to resist the feel of her tight body gripping and squeezing around me.

Chapter Six

Olivia

Ho. Ly. Shit.

Abruptly boneless, I collapse back onto the cushions, hot and sweaty and out of breath. Noah's mouth just blew my mind all over our living room sofa. I'm still trembling with the intensity of my release.

Noah sits back on his heels, smirking like the cat who ate the canary. *Well, eating and pussies were involved, but not quite in that way* . . . He makes a show of licking his bottom lip and then wiping his mouth on his sleeve.

"Wow, Snowflake. Did that feel as good as you taste? It sure as hell sounded like it."

My brain is too scrambled to come up with a snappy retort. Or any coherent words whatsoever, really. I just nod slowly at him, admiring him anew, like he's not just Noah anymore but some strange, exotic species I've never encountered before. And shit, maybe I haven't. Just the man's tongue sent me into a spiraling orgasm so strong I saw stars.

His grin broadens. Damn, he looks so good, I don't even care that I'm stroking his already overinflated ego. His handsome face is flushed, his dark eyes dilated and heavy-lidded, his hair mussed from where my fingers tangled in it. And if I look down, I can see an obvious bulge straining against the zipper of his slacks—complete with a wet spot at the tip.

Kneeling up, he slides his trim, toned waist between my thighs until our chests are pressed together. His damp lips brush the shell of my ear as he murmurs, "If you want it, there's more where that came from."

His clothed erection rubs into my bare, oversensitized clit and I gasp aloud. Unbelievably, a tendril of new heat curls through me.

I just had the orgasm to end all orgasms, but part of me *does* want more. I want to touch Noah. I want to feel our bodies moving together. I want that huge cock inside me, fucking me until I can't walk straight. I want to see him come undone—it's only fair, isn't it? He got to watch *me* while I melted into a babbling, shaking puddle.

Almost of its own accord, my mouth opens to reply. The potential for enormous pleasure rests on the tip of my tongue. Tonight can go so much further, and all I have to do is reach out for him . . .

But then what will happen? What will "more" mean in the morning?

This is far from the first time that sleeping with Noah has crossed my mind. How can it be, with a sex god strutting around me all day every day? But now that the moment has actually arrived, staring me in the face, I find myself shrinking away from it. If I say yes, there's no going back from this decision. That awareness paralyzes me with uncertainty. What if I lose my head, my heart, my company? All over a man . . . who's a known player.

Now that I've started overthinking, I can't stop. As far as I can tell, there are only two possible outcomes. Either tonight is just casual fun, where we're nothing more than fuck buddies, or . . . sex will change everything between us. I don't know how I feel about either option. I'm not ready for love, but I don't like the idea of non-committed screwing either.

And then there's the matter of how we came to be here in the first place. We're in an arranged marriage, for Christ's sake. Maybe our emotions have developed along the way, but that doesn't change the fact that our relationship was originally rooted in business. This isn't real. It almost feels like we're using each other—even though it's for the greater good, we're still sacrificing our chances of finding real love with our real soul mates in the future while we each play the role we're supposed to.

Things have already gotten way out of hand. Fuck . . . tonight was a mistake. I never should have let Noah tempt me. I should have told him to knock it off, and gone to bed.

I've paused for too long. Sensing my hesitation, Noah pulls back to look into my eyes. "You okay?"

I resist the impulse to drop my gaze. "Yeah. I just . . . I'm not sure."

Noah is silent for a moment. Almost, anyway; he's close enough for me to hear him sigh through his nose. As if he's debating something with himself.

Finally, he says, "Then let's stop."

"But you never got a chance to . . ." I can still feel that huge, rock-hard bulge against my inner thigh.

"Hey, I'm a big boy. I can take care of myself." He winks at me.

Oh, believe me, I know. My cheeks heat up, remembering what happened the last time I left him unsatisfied. But there's a strained note in his voice, and I can't help feeling guilty.

"I'm sorry," I say reflexively. This isn't fair. He made an effort to put together this cute date night, he gave me one of the best orgasms I've ever had, and now I won't return the favor. I'm just going to leave him with blue balls. *God, I feel like a royal bitch.*

His reply comes quick and sharp. "Hey. Never apologize. I don't want anything to happen just because you feel obligated." Before I can blink, his serious tone melts away and he gives me his cockiest smirk. "Noah Tate doesn't need pity fucks. When we finally do this . . ." His lips graze my neck, one last kiss, and I shiver. "I want it to be because you're begging for it. For me."

Then he pulls away to stand up and help me to my feet. I sway a little, still slightly unsteady. Jesus, that orgasm floored me. Maybe I should change my mind again . . .

No, I can't. I'm not ready for more. Definitely not yet, possibly not ever.

We get ready for bed, both of us quiet. As I brush my teeth, I tell myself firmly that I made the right decision. As fun as tonight was, it will be better for us to keep our laser focus on business.

And unlike our first night at our new penthouse, I'll plug my ears and not go snooping around if Noah's out of bed for too long. This time I'll know exactly what he's doing.

Am I a bad wife? I shouldn't care so much—it's not like I ever wanted to be his wife in the first place. But like it or not, we're married. And Noah is my friend. Whatever our legal relationship is, I owe him what friends owe each other.

How does Noah feel about what happened tonight? He backed off so quickly. I know he'd never pressure me into sex or make me feel obligated, but I expected a little more good-natured grumpiness. He did sound frustrated, but something about it felt different from the other times I've shot him down before. Almost like he was . . . ashamed? Did he think he'd hurt or scared me? Or was it just because we'd been drinking? The idea that both Noah and I might feel guilty about this doesn't make me feel better.

I sigh. Tonight's pleasant atmosphere has turned so sour so quickly. I have no idea what to feel here. I wish . . .

I wish Mom were still alive.

She'd be able to give me advice. She would know how a marriage is supposed to work. How to be a good wife. Dad can tell me his side of their story, but there are some things a woman can only ask another woman about. And Camryn's just as inexperienced with marriage as I am.

Noah and I get under the covers, facing opposite directions. The few feet separating us feels like a mile. I curl up on my side of the bed, lying still and silent, and wait for sleep to take me out of this awkward situation.

• • •

The next day at work, I've engaged full ice-queen mode. I have to keep my defenses firmly in place, but somber thoughts from last night keep playing through my mind. As sexy as Noah is, as incredible as he made me feel, I can't let anything distract me. All business, no nonsense.

If I start sleeping with Noah, who knows how my feelings might change? Office romances are risky for a reason . . . someone always gets hurt, and then the workplace atmosphere is ruined. *No fucking thank you.* Saving Tate & Cane takes top priority. My life has enough stress without adding in all the emotional entanglements that come with sex.

I'm not overthinking this, I tell myself yet again as I rinse out my coffee mug in the break room's sink. *It's the right decision.*

Someone taps me on the shoulder. "You have a minute?" Noah's voice asks.

Crap . . . just who I wanted to deal with right now, the center of all my turmoil. But I keep my tone cool and professional as I turn around. "Yes? What is it?"

"Remember how I played a few rounds of golf with Red Dog's CMO last week?" When I nod at him, Noah says, "He offered to refer us a new client."

Something about Noah's tone makes me frown. "Then why don't you seem happy?"

"Well, he put me in touch with their campaign project leader and I talked to him—"

"You accepted his referral without asking me?" I blurt, interrupting him. By now he ought to know how much I hate being out of the loop.

"Relax. I was just putting out a feeler, nothing that would imply we'd take the gig. Anyway, they're definitely a big fish. Willing to pay very well . . . but they would want us to partner with their in-house marketing staff."

"Oh, Christ." That would take away our creative autonomy and clog everything up with bureaucracy and constant check-ins. "Why even contract with an outside firm if you're just going to hamstring them?"

"Maybe this new client is a control freak."

I pointedly ignore Noah's teasing wink. "In my opinion, you should find a nice way to tell them to go fuck themselves."

"I don't know about that," he says with a shrug. "We stand to make a lot of money."

"We also stand to waste a lot of time and effort wrestling with their bullshit restrictions. These guys clearly don't trust the judgment they're paying for—and that's a big red flag. We have other prospective clients who'll yield better returns on our investment."

"We don't know for sure that the referral is bad news. And if we can play nice with their peanut gallery for this project, maybe they'll let us have more freedom in the future."

"You wanted my opinion and now you have it. Do whatever you feel like." Normally I would keep arguing my point, but I just want Noah out of my hair so I can go hide in my office and get my mind off last night's awkwardness.

"Duly noted." Noah's lips quirk into a mischievous

half smile. "I know I've said this before, Snowflake, but you're cute when you're a hard-ass."

"Then I guess I'm always cute. Glad we can agree on something," I retort frostily. I regret the words as soon as they're out of my mouth. Shit, I meant to cut him off at the knees, but I got sucked into his stupid flirtation game instead. Why does that always happen?

Before I can anticipate it, Noah darts in for a peck on my lips. My mouth drops open and I stare at him, blinking wide-eyed. Over his shoulder, I can see Dad passing by. He pauses to give us a fond smile, as if to say, *Ah, young love . . . how sweet.*

Fuck no. Noah does *not* get to manipulate the situation like this. He can't derail our conversations whenever he gets bored. He can't dismiss my concerns like I'm just some silly girl playing Business Barbie. And kissing me in front of Dad makes me uncomfortable. It's too much PDA for the office. It's too much PDA for my family. And it's too much PDA for my current state of mind—confused, conflicted, defensive, maybe even a little scared, if I'm being totally honest.

Drawing myself up, I give Noah my best

disapproving scowl.

My annoyance deepens when Noah's only reaction is a quizzical blink. Like he has no idea what I mean. Like I'm acting crazy and he's being the reasonable one.

"I'm trying to have an important discussion with you, and you're not taking me seriously. Besides, I don't like PDA."

He raises his hands slightly in a gesture of mock surrender. "Jeez, Snowflake, I was just playing around. What's the problem? I didn't think you'd still be wound so tight . . ." He lets the end of that thought—*after last night*—go unspoken. Which is good, because if he ever talked about our sex life at work, I might just have to kill him.

I scoff. "Right, as if one little O would turn me into your swooning cheerleader. It takes a lot more than that to make me fall—" I stop myself before I say *in love*.

He cocks his head, then shrugs. "A man can dream. But I'm offended that you called it just a little O." His voice drops, all low and silky. "The way you were screaming and clawing my back . . . I could tell that wasn't *little*. They probably felt the aftershocks in China."

I'm stunned. I open and close my mouth, but nothing comes out.

"Call me unprofessional if you want. I'm willing to dial things back during the workday. But nighttime is for fun, and you can't deny that you had a whole hell of a lot."

I finally find my voice. "I hate to cut you off there, *Mr. Tate*," I huff, "but some of us don't have time to play grab-ass all day."

Without giving him a chance to respond, I turn on my heel and storm away. This drama is just too much to deal with, especially on top of my responsibilities and deadlines.

I shut myself away in the safe, peaceful cloister of my office, intent on getting some serious work done and forgetting all about Noah. But almost an hour later, I haven't accomplished anything. I've just been staring blankly at my computer screen, not registering any of the words or numbers or figures, utterly lost in thought.

Noah is a confusing, sexy jerk-face. However, as much as I hate to give him any points, he's right about one thing—I can't deny that last night was amazing. And the longer I think about it, the less sense it makes to even try denying it, and the more I wonder . . .

Why am I fighting this?

The only man I've ever slept with was Brad, and those encounters were always boring at best and horrible at worst. Poking at my insides with his little stick while I tried to climax and failed miserably. Maybe my bad experiences have made me more skittish than it's reasonable to be.

If last night was anything to go by, Noah is clearly determined to get me off. And he knows exactly what he's doing in the bedroom. *If he's that good with his mouth, I can only imagine* . . . Just the memory makes me feel a little too warm. Noah can easily make up for all my years of no sex and bad sex, frustration and inexperience.

And we're stuck with each other for the foreseeable future. At the very least, we'll have to keep up this marriage charade long enough to get the company back on stable footing and turn it profitable again, which will be no small feat. It can take months. Long, grueling hours, incredible pressure, exhaustion, and stress. Why not take advantage of the fact that we're in this situation together? Why shouldn't I have a treat to look forward to at the end of the workday?

Sex has been on the horizon from the beginning. We've already experimented with making out, and that went pretty great. I won't even have to swallow my pride—not too much, anyway—since Noah's bet about seducing me in four days has long since expired.

So, what exactly am I waiting for? What's the point of a "trial period" that never graduates into the real thing? And when have I ever gotten anywhere in life by hanging back? Sure, I'm hardly a daredevil like Noah, but there's a difference between reasonable caution and paranoia. If I always play everything so safe, nothing will ever change. I'll just be stuck in neutral forever. I need to take the plunge. Toss off my big-girl panties and just say *screw it* for once.

I give myself a decisive nod to cement my resolve. So . . . that's that. I'm going to start fucking my husband. There, I said it. I'm going to enjoy some marital sex. I'm a mature, responsible woman—I can totally handle this. And I can always call the whole thing off if I try it and I don't like where it's going.

Someday, I still want my soul mate and my happily-ever-after romance. But that true love story isn't going to happen anytime soon. Right here, right now, what I have is Noah. And that's nothing to sneeze at. He's one of the hottest men I've ever met, and more importantly, he's good to me. Our friendship is solid; I trust him to show me a fun time and never hurt me.

What's the worst that can happen? With that thought in mind, I set out for Noah's office, my heart beating fast and hard.

He's left his door wide open. When I peek in to see him sitting at his desk, he glances at me over the top of his computer screen.

"You need something?" he asks.

I come inside, closing the door behind me. This is definitely going to be the strangest proposal I've ever made at work. Taking a deep breath, I face Noah with as much cool confidence as I can muster.

"So," I say casually, "I've been thinking. Maybe that orgasm wasn't so bad after all . . ."

Chapter Seven

Noah

Barely an hour after she tore me a new asshole and stormed off, Olivia is standing in front of my desk. And underneath her nervousness is a mischievous glint in her eye.

"No?" I tease her, pretending to be surprised. "I thought you said it was just a little O earlier."

She shakes her head. There's a tiny crease between her brows, and I know that whatever she's about to propose, she's given it a lot of thought.

I rise to my feet and come around the desk so we're standing facing each other. I can't help pushing her buttons a little more. "Excellent, because there's plenty more where that came from." I love when she blushes. She looks beautiful when she's fully relaxed and carefree. This is my favorite version of her.

"That's good, because I've been thinking. Maybe this whole husband arrangement might come in handy,"

Olivia says.

"Indeed it can. I have a big dick and I know how to use it. We've proven that even you, Snowflake, like orgasms. We have six hours between when we get off work and bedtime . . . that's more than enough time to make you scream my name."

"God, you're crude." Her cheeks flush even pinker.

Bingo.

"How would you prefer I behave, Olivia? Like your little lapdog from accounting, polite and well-mannered and hanging on your every word? You'll have to neuter me first."

She raises her chin. She didn't think I noticed that shriveled prick sniffing around, but I did.

"Sorry, Snowflake, but I'm a man. A speak-my-mind, fight-for-what-I-believe, bleed-for-my-country, red-meat-eating man. I don't bow down to anyone. You want to fuck around and blow off some steam? Fine. It'll be fun. But I'm not handing my balls over to you."

She rolls her eyes. "Just don't talk and we'll be

fine."

I chuckle. It's so fun to see her flustered.

"No, seriously, don't speak."

Nodding, I make a show of tightening my lips and zipping them shut.

Even I'm smart enough to know when to stay quiet. And when sex with Olivia is on the line, I'm more than willing to play along. All this teasing banter is melting my little snowflake, slowly but surely . . . just according to plan.

• • •

"What is all of this? I'm pretty much a sure bet. You understand that, right?" Olivia's tone is amused, maybe even a little chastising. But there's a huge smile on her face.

I asked her on an official date tonight. I've filled our penthouse with pale pink peonies from floor to ceiling—every counter and table topped with a crystal vase or a small water bowl of fragrant blossoms. I've even drawn her a bath with petals floating on the warm water.

"We're not really dating. You didn't have to do this," she says, her tone teasing. "It's just business. And sex. That's it."

I won't admit it, but I'm a little hurt. If I did all this for any other woman, she'd be impressed and dazzled. But winning over Olivia is a challenge unlike any other.

"Go get ready. We have a seven-thirty reservation." I give her ass a playful swat.

"Yes, sir," she murmurs, sauntering past me.

Damn . . . I'm sure she only meant that sarcastically, but I like hearing those words more than I ever imagined.

Olivia heads into the master bath, and I hear her soft groan when she sinks into the water.

Knowing she's undressed on just the other side of that door is sweet torture. But she's told me she's ready for sex, and that means I need to do the right thing— tell her about the heir clause in the contract.

While she bathes, primps, and dresses, I wait in the

living room, trying to get my thoughts in order. Tonight might be the most important conversation I've ever had. The future of Tate & Cane depends on how carefully I can break this news to her.

But then she steps out from the bedroom and I forget how to breathe, let alone form coherent sentences.

"Wow. You look . . ."

"Is this okay?" She spins, treating me to the 360-degree view.

The knee-length dress is modestly cut in the front, not showing too much leg, or really any cleavage. But the back plunges all the way down to just above her ass. And the deep wine color contrasts with her milky skin beautifully.

Sweet Jesus.

"You look edible," I stammer out.

A sly grin spreads across her berry-stained lips. "Edible?"

So much for being smooth and playing it cool.

"They'll be plenty of time for that later," I say, recovering only slightly from the sight of her. "Are you ready?"

"Yes, but you still haven't told me where we're going."

My cell phone chimes and I check the notification. "The car's here. Come on. I'll tell you on the way."

I take her hand and guide her to the door, where she picks up a little silver purse and a tube of lipstick.

When we reach the street in front of the penthouse, Olivia pauses on the sidewalk. "You got a limo?"

I open the door to the sleek black town car and nod. "It's a special occasion." Olivia slips inside and I lean down to meet her eyes. "Plus I'll be able to feel you up without crashing the car." I grin.

Olivia chuckles, warm and deep, and the sound goes straight to my head. I love putting a smile on her face. Honestly though, not driving means I can focus one hundred percent on Olivia.

Tonight will be more than just the first time we have sex. Tonight is the first time I'm going to be intimate with my wife. *My wife.* Shit, I'm still not used to that—both the idea of having a wife and the idea that it's Olivia. But I take this shit seriously. Tonight means much more than just some random hookup. I really like Olivia. I want us to work. Plus, I haven't fucked anyone in months. My body is more than ready for this.

She slips inside the car and I climb in behind her. Since I've already given the driver tonight's agenda, he whisks us away without a word.

After dinner at a nice seafood restaurant where we enjoyed lobster and wine and shared the lemon cheesecake for dessert, Olivia and I visit one of the city's best jazz clubs, seated at a tiny round table for two with a perfect view of the stage.

She reaches over and squeezes my hand while the band warms up. "Thank you. I can't believe you planned all this."

I shrug. "It's nothing."

She frowns. "It's not *nothing.* Believe me when I say

that no man has ever planned a date this extravagant."

Never? That simultaneously relieves me and pisses me off a little. I'm glad that she's impressed, but it's a damn tragedy that she's never been romanced properly. Of course Olivia deserves all this—and more.

"Well, you're stuck with me now, babe."

She chews on her lower lip, and for the briefest flash of a moment, I read the hesitation on her features. I might not have been who she'd choose as a husband, but that didn't change the outcome. Whatever happens next, wherever we go in life, I will always be her first husband. Part of me hopes I'll be her one-and-only husband, as crazy as that sounds.

During dinner, the conversation flowed well. True, we did talk mostly about work, but it was the type of gossipy small talk that kept us both laughing. And now, we're each on our third glass of wine, and the soft jazz music floating through the air has created an undeniably romantic atmosphere.

Olivia has a subtle smile painted across her lips as she looks out over the stage. But despite the perfect evening, I can't escape the thoughts that have lingered in the back of my head all evening. The guilt stewing inside me has reached a boiling point. As much as I want to just enjoy our date, I can't put it off any longer. I need to tell Olivia about the baby-making that's supposed to happen. Like, now.

"Olivia, I . . ."

She reaches over and touches my hand. "Dance with me?" Her eyes are filled with a hopeful longing that I never thought I'd see her direct at me. I find myself nodding and rising to my feet.

Then we're swaying on the dance floor—her fingertips on the back of my neck, her sweet honeysuckle scent surrounding me, my hands molded to the curve of her hips like they were made to fit there. And I . . . just can't. Not right now. This moment is too perfect to ruin.

It seems like she's finally starting to warm to me, to the idea of us. I promise myself that I'll tell her as soon as we get home. For now, I push the words I need to say down my throat, and I just hold her.

• • •

The instant the penthouse door closes behind us, Olivia's lips are on my throat and her hand is on my cock.

Hello there, instant hard-on.

"Whoa. Slow down, baby. We have all night." I grip her wrist, drawing her hand away from my cock. *Plus, we still need to talk. We have to.*

"Fuck going slow. I've gone slow my entire life. I overthink every decision to death. I haven't had sex in . . ." She pauses and looks down. "Years."

"Years?" I don't mean to blurt it with such force, but holy hell. *Seriously?*

She frowns. "Don't make fun."

I touch her cheek softly. "I'm not." Then I lean in for a chaste kiss. "I just want to make this good for you."

"You will." She kisses me back. "I have no doubts about that."

And then her hands are on my dick again, and I couldn't stop her even if I wanted to. She's unbuckling my belt, tugging down my zipper, shoving her hands inside my boxers to palm my erection. Her hands are so delicate, so warm, and it's the first time she's touched me.

"Christ, Olivia." I grunt, pushing my pants down my hips so she can stroke me freely.

Is marital sex hotter than hookup sex? The answer to that question seems to be a big fucking *YES*. Because just the thought of banging my wife has me harder than ever before. So hard that my cock is leaking pre-cum from the tip, something Olivia seems to have noticed. She rubs her thumb along the head, smearing the warm fluid against my sensitive skin, making me groan.

I look down between us to where Olivia's gaze is glued as well. Her hand moves up and down my shaft with a firm, yet tender grip.

"You're so big, so sexy," she murmurs.

"That's right, baby. Now stroke that big cock."

I take her mouth in a hungry kiss, our tongues

dueling as her hands slide up and down. Oh God, I can't think, but I need to stop this. Man up and push her off. Tell her what's on my mind.

Instead, what do I do? I pet her cheek with my thumb and say, "Get down on your knees and put your mouth on me, baby." I've fantasized about Olivia's sassy mouth wrapped around my cock for so long, this is sure to be a dream come true.

Without a trace of the hesitation I expected, she drops to her knees before me and grips my base with both hands.

I don't ask her to suck it, because unless she's secretly a blow job expert—or she can unhinge her jaw—I doubt I'll fit in her mouth. So instead I stroke her hair, and caress her cheek, and watch her lick me like a lollipop and swirl her tongue around the tip. Her efforts are cute. And the languid, wet kiss she leaves on the crown feels incredible. She murmurs little enticing noises as I pet her hair. She fits the tip of me in her mouth and suckles lightly, making me groan.

Hauling her up to her feet, I kiss her one more time. "Let's take this to the bedroom."

She nods eagerly and turns to walk ahead of me, swinging her hips in that backless dress.

I can't believe she's mine. Can't believe that she's about to give herself to me. A flash of pride tinged with guilt whips through me, and I give chase.

In the bedroom, Olivia watches me as she lets the straps of her dress fall down her shoulders, until the whole thing is just a puddle of fabric at her feet. Having forgone a bra, she's left standing in a lacy black thong and her black stiletto heels.

"So fucking sexy." I groan, stopping in front of her to kiss her lips and then her neck.

My pants are still open in the front, and Olivia reaches inside to take me in her hands again.

"Christ, woman." I'm putty in her hands. Whatever she wants to do, I'm game. But I can't give her all the control. "On the bed," I growl, taking a step back.

Olivia obeys, stepping out of her heels and moving to lie down in the center of the bed. *Our* bed. Shit, that's going to take some getting used to. It should make me nervous that this woman will be here when I wake up, that this isn't just another one-night stand. If I fuck this up, if things change and get weird after, there will be no escaping Olivia.

Strangely, though, that isn't what's making me nervous.

It's the sweetly hopeful way Olivia's wide blue eyes are watching me. She wants this erotic experience with me, wants to experience all the pleasure I can show her. But what if this encounter goes the way it's supposed to and she ends up pregnant? What then? Are we ready for a baby? Are we even cut out to be parents? Will she hate me?

But the time to talk has passed. I blew all my chances to talk about the heir clause tonight; I'll just have to tell her tomorrow. Because right now Olivia is waiting for me, and I've never left a woman in need.

Pushing all those troubling thoughts of babies from my brain, I strip, then lie down beside Olivia so we're facing each other.

"Are you nervous?" I ask her, stroking her cheek, trying to get back into the moment.

She gives me a careful nod. "That's stupid, right? We're married now."

"Nothing you're feeling is stupid."

She smiles at me. "It's just . . . been a while."

I caress her upper arms, unable to stop touching her. She looks so sexy lying here in just her thong, looking at me like I'm the big bad wolf who's ready to eat her up.

"We can go slow," I murmur, my lips on hers.

"Okay." She nods, kissing me back.

In the moonlit room, we lie side by side, our arms and legs intertwined, kissing for a long time. My tongue explores her mouth and she matches my eager pace, meeting me lick for lick. Her tongue tastes of champagne, and I'm having a hell of a time holding myself back from stripping off her panties and diving between her legs. The taste I had last night wasn't enough. When it comes to Olivia, nothing can ever be enough.

A sound of frustration rises up her throat. "We

don't have to go *that* slow."

"No?" I chuckle. *Thank fucking God.* I peel her thong down her legs and toss it over the side of the bed. "My kind of woman."

I shift closer and part her legs, sliding her top knee over my hip, so she's open for me. Then I rub the head of my cock over her clit, coating myself in her warmth and making her moan at the contact.

"That feels so good, Noah," she cries, circling her hips, pushing herself closer.

"Need to make sure you're ready for me."

I bury my face against her neck, breathing in her familiar scent while I push one long finger inside her. She's snug, and I take my time adding another finger before slowly withdrawing.

She reaches up to palm my cheek, feeling the stubble on my jaw. Her eyes never leave mine as I pump my fingers in and out.

"I want you, Noah."

Her voice is just a whisper, and when I look in her

eyes, I see the amount of courage it takes her to admit that. She's been so strong, so resolute for so long, that sex will only complicate our business arrangement. I have no idea what changed her mind. Okay, so I have some idea—it could have been that orgasm I delivered the other night. There's plenty more where that came from.

Just do it. "I know, baby. Soon. Nice and easy . . ."

I line myself up, shuddering at how warm and soft her wet opening feels on the tip of my cock. Easing in just an inch, I bite back a groan. Her body grips mine so tightly, it's perfection.

Everything inside me wants to pump her full of my cum and watch her squirm, breathless as she comes down from the multiple orgasms I know I can give her. Instead my brain is screaming at me to stop this. To tell her the truth.

"Wait," she says, placing one hand on my chest.

I'm almost relieved when she stops us. "What's wrong?"

"Don't we need a condom? I'm not on birth

control."

"I . . ."

My heart is pounding and I feel light-headed, almost dizzy. Whether it's because I'm desperate to feel her around me, or because I'm not cut out for the deception and devastation that lies ahead, I have no idea.

"I can't do this," I bite out.

"What? Why not?" Olivia sits up, peering down at me with confusion all over her features.

I look away. "I just can't," I repeat uselessly, unable to think of anything else.

"If this is about the condoms, I'll run down to the drugstore. It'll take ten minutes. Fifteen tops." Her voice rises in concern.

I shake my head. "I'm sorry. I'm suddenly not feeling well."

That's not a total lie; my stomach is certainly churning. I climb out of bed and grab my boxers from the floor, slipping them on while Olivia scowls at me.

"What the hell, Noah?"

I don't reply; I just grab my pillow from the bed and head to the couch. It's going to be a long fucking night.

• • •

"So let me get this straight?" Sterling says around a mouthful of pancakes. "You feigned a headache like a bitter old housewife instead of fucking her?"

I jab my fork at my eggs, stabbing the runny yolks, my appetite gone. Of course I wasn't sick last night. It was an attack of shame and regret.

"I couldn't do it."

Sterling shakes his head. "Of course you couldn't. You need to stop behaving like a grunting caveman and talk with her about the contract. Use your words and have a real conversation about this. Which has been my position since the wedding, I'll remind you." He waves his fork at me for emphasis.

"Yeah, yeah. Shut it." I take a sip of my tea while Sterling continues eating. At least one of us has an appetite.

After a sleepless night spent tossing and turning on the couch, I got up early and asked Sterling out to breakfast before work. We've never met up so early before, but he practically jumped at the invitation. He knew from the start that my arranged marriage was going to implode, and I think the bastard just wants a front-row seat.

"I don't even know if she likes kids, if she wants kids," I muse out loud.

"Yeah, that's a problem."

Damn him for always being the voice of reason. He makes all my conundrums sound so simple and obvious.

What I'm starting to realize is that there's the spark of something more between Olivia and me. I can't deceive any woman about this, but especially not Olivia. She isn't just a means to an end. We can have the seeds of a real relationship here, and I'm not ready to fuck up that possibility.

At the same time, though . . . the fate of our entire company is still at stake. How do I protect both Olivia and Tate & Cane? How do I convince her?

I toss some cash onto the table and stand, unable to stomach any more. "I've got to get to the office. Thanks for the chat."

"Anytime you need a therapy session, I'm here." Smiling, Sterling gives me a wave before digging back into his pancakes.

When I arrive at work, I go to the one place I know Olivia won't find me.

"Hey, Rosita," I call, clearing off a countertop in the mailroom and sitting down.

"I've missed you, *mi amor*," she says, wheeling a cart full of packages over. As she approaches, she makes a *tsking* sound under her breath. Then she stops in front of me and runs her thumb under my eye. "You don't look well. These dark circles aren't normally here."

I shrug. "I didn't get much sleep last night."

"Oh?" She gives me a knowing smile.

"No, nothing like that." I guess I need to preface my statement; otherwise, people are likely to think I was burning up the sheets with my blushing bride. We are newlyweds, after all. "I slept on the couch last night."

Her expression instantly falls. Frowning, she gives my cheek a pat. Then she lowers herself into the chair across from me. "Tell Mama Rosie all about it."

"Things between me and Olivia are good ... they're just kind of complicated."

"Complicated how?" Rosita raises her eyebrows.

"How did you know you wanted kids?"

From her surprised expression, that's clearly not the topic she was expecting. "I don't know. I guess I always just knew from the time I was small that I wanted to be a mother."

I nod. Makes sense. I think women just know. They have that maternal instinct, that ticking biological clock. Only I don't know if Olivia feels that way.

"Do you want children? Is that what this is about?" Rosita asks in her calm, yet confident voice.

I *have* always wanted at least one kid, hopefully two. But this situation isn't about what either of us want. Our know-it-all, matchmaking fathers thought it best that we start a family in order to take over their massive corporation, and now I'm feeling the pressure of putting a bun in Olivia's oven ASAP.

Does Rosita really need all that background information, though?

Deciding to keep this conversation as simple as possible, I just answer, "Yeah. But I don't know how Olivia feels."

Rosita smiles warmly at me and rises to pat the back of my hand. "You have plenty of time. The ink is barely dry on your marriage certificate. Enjoy life with just the two of you for a few years first. Once kids come, you can never go back. This time is precious."

The sour feeling in the pit of my stomach intensifies. Great . . . yet another reason why everything in my life is fucked. Not what I need to hear right now. But Rosita doesn't know that, so I nod and force a smile at her, as if her wise advice perfectly hit the spot.

"Thanks for the talk, Rosie. I better get back to work."

"Anytime," she calls after me.

Now I just have to figure out what the fuck I'm supposed to do.

Chapter Eight

Olivia

What the hell happened last night? I worked so hard to psych myself up for sex, and *Noah* was the one who got cold feet? Unbelievable. The man can never stop flirting with me or bragging about how amazing he is in bed, but when the time came to put his money where his mouth was . . . actually, his mouth didn't go anywhere either.

And I can't even ask Noah about it, because I can't *find* him. I woke up to an empty bed, with no sign of my husband anywhere in the apartment. He wasn't in his office when I arrived at work either.

All damn day, I've been trying to catch him alone. He won't answer any of my calls or texts or e-mails, and his secretary keeps saying "oh, bad luck, you just missed him" every time I stop by her desk.

Is it really bad luck, though? Is his jam-packed schedule today just an annoying coincidence? Or . . . is he avoiding me on purpose?

I stomp down the little voice in the back of my head that whispers, *He's changed his mind about you. He finally came to his senses, realized what a huge mistake this relationship is. He regrets everything. He doesn't want to touch you or even talk to you.* That poisonous hiss sounds an awful lot like Brad, and I'm done with him for good.

But God, I'm still so confused and frustrated. I was all set to confront my sexual hang-ups, and then our showdown was canceled at the last possible second.

Dammit, I refuse to let my emotional effort go to waste. I'm going to be brave and get laid if it's the last thing I do. But first, I'm going to find out why Noah suddenly abandoned ship last night. And if I can't track down the slippery SOB at work, I'll just corner him tonight. He has to come home sometime, right?

• • •

Just as I'm folding a sheet of office paper into a voodoo doll and preparing to repeatedly stab it in the crotch, Camryn swings by my office.

"Hey, what's up?" I ask as she slides into the chair

in front of my desk.

"Not much." She shrugs. "I wanted to see if you wanted to grab an early lunch."

I glance at the clock and see it's only half past eleven, but yes, getting out of this building and escaping the rejection burning through my veins is exactly what I need. "I would eat dog shit right now if I meant I got an hour's worth of girl time with you."

Camryn's cheery expression falls. "Well, I'm not real keen on eating dog shit, so why don't you tell me what happened, sweetie?"

I huff out a sigh and rise to my feet. "I'll tell you all about it over lunch."

And I do. Over chicken strips and fries (nothing says comfort food like deep-fried anything dipped in generous amounts of ranch dressing), I lay it all out on the table. All my baggage. All the pain and hurt and doubt Noah caused me last night.

"He had me convinced that he wanted me, wooed me, was on his best, most charming behavior, and then bam! Nothing." I lick the grease from my fingers and take a big gulp of soda to wash down my lunch.

"What a twat," she grumbles, nodding to encourage me along.

"He slept on the couch and was gone before I got up this morning, so obviously he's avoiding me like he knows he did something wrong." I freeze, my straw halfway to my lips.

"What?" Camryn asks.

"Unless I'm the one who did something wrong."

This earns me a confused look. "Do you think you did something wrong?"

I shrug. "Maybe I shouldn't have told him that it had been so long."

"Noah isn't like that. He wouldn't care."

Camryn's right. I replay the evening in my head. Dinner. Champagne. Dancing. Flirting. Laughing. Groping.

"Maybe I was too aggressive. I had my hand in his pants the second the door closed." I push my hands into my hair, remembering how I acted, in all my horny glory. "The lock didn't even click into place and I was all up in his business. I started giving him a blow job in the damn foyer of our apartment."

"That's hot," she commented, taking another bite of her food. "What guy doesn't want a blow job in the foyer?"

I don't know. Apparently Noah. But he's been practically begging to show me his dick . . . I frown, unsure if my actions last night somehow caused him to pull away.

She leans toward me, her eyes full of sweet pity. "Sweetie, if you're sucking his dick, you can do it anywhere, anytime, and it's okay. It's almost a rule."

The worst part of this whole situation is the growing seed of doubt he left. *What's wrong with me? Why wasn't I good enough?*

"What happened next?" she asks.

"He took me into the bedroom and stripped me down. We were kissing." God, the kissing. The man can do incredible things with his tongue. "And then he was rubbing his . . . *anaconda* . . . all over my . . . *honey pot*, and I mentioned something about a condom."

"Hmm." She looks as perplexed as I feel. "Please tell me you didn't use the word honey pot?"

Shaking my head, I continue. "No. But maybe it was me. Maybe my vagina's ugly?"

The guy seated next to us whips his head in my direction so fast, I'm surprised he doesn't get whiplash.

Camryn pats my hand. "There is absolutely nothing wrong with your vagina. I'm sure of it."

"Then why, Cam? Why? Why would he do that? Because I don't believe for one second that he was all of a sudden ill."

She shakes her head. "No, neither do I." She sets her fork down next to her Cobb salad. "Do you really want to know what I think?"

My stomach tightening, I nod.

She wipes her mouth with her napkin and leans forward. "I think it hit Noah that this unique situation with you isn't what he's used to. This isn't a random hookup, or a booty call that he can duck out on in the morning. Whether you guys like it or not, sex between the two of you is going to mean something."

I frown and chew on my thumbnail. "In what way?"

"You're a married couple now."

I roll my eyes. "It's a business agreement. An arranged marriage. And I proposed we be fuck buddies since we're stuck together. It's not some romantic till-death-do-us-part, lovey-dovey marriage."

Camryn holds up her palms. "All I'm saying is sex for men isn't just physical like we sometimes like to believe. And I think something spooked Noah—got into his head."

"That's ridiculous." *But is it?* Aren't those some of the same things I was worried about? My whole objection for us having naked fun in the first place?

"Ridiculous or not, I want you to know that his backing out had nothing to do with you, and everything to do with something going on inside his head."

"So, what do I do now?"

She grins wickedly. "That all depends. Do you still want to bang him?"

Stupid question. Is the value of pi 3.14? Does my husband have a horse cock? *Yes* to all of the above.

"More than anything." I grin back at her, my expression equally cheeky.

Camryn cracks up laughing. "Okay, then here's what you do . . ."

• • •

Later, back at the office, I'm working away when my head snaps up. Walking past my window—was that Noah just now? I jump out of my chair and peek around the doorjamb. *Yep . . . I'd recognize that ass anywhere.* He turns the corner and I follow him at what I hope is a casual distance. Time to confront him, just like Camryn suggested.

When I reach Noah's office, his door is shut and locked. But the lights are on and I can see the silhouette of his head through the frosted glass window. It doesn't look like he's on the phone or having a private meeting with anyone.

I give his door three loud raps. "Hey, Noah."

No answer. So he's being stubborn. Too bad; I can be stubborn too. I knock again and call, "I know you're in there. I need to talk to you."

The door flies open. Noah looks irritated. Well, good—I guess that makes two of us.

"Something better be on fire," he snaps.

I keep my eyes steady on his. "Sorry, but no. And we should talk in private."

His mouth presses into a firm line, but he steps aside to let me walk into his office.

I shut the door behind me and turn to face him. "So ... about last night. Care to tell me what happened?"

He folds his arms over his chest. "Weren't you there? You already know."

"No, I really don't." Straightening my back—I

can't match his height, but I'll still try—I plant my hands on my hips. "The date, the dancing, the wooing . . . and then the bailing."

"I told you I wasn't feeling well."

"Really? Because you don't look sick to me right now." And if he *was* sick last night, then why sleep on the couch? No way. Not buying it.

Noah throws up his hands. "Maybe it was something I ate at dinner. Maybe I just got a headache. What's with the damn third degree?"

Then he drops his gaze. It was only for a second, but I saw it, and I know evasive maneuvers when I see them. So I press harder.

"It really seemed to me like you were scared of having sex."

He blinks, his mouth open, then forces a laugh. "What? We're still talking about me, right? You're always sniping at me for . . . how did you put it? Fucking half of New York City?"

"But I'm not your typical conquest. I'm your *wife*.

Correct me if I'm wrong, but your style tends more toward 'wham, bam, thank you, ma'am' than 'until death do us part.'" I pause to raise my eyebrows at him for emphasis. "Last night wasn't going to be just a casual screw where you forgot my name five minutes later. I think you backed off because you were worried that sex would make things too real between us. You're scared you might feel something for me."

For a moment, he just stares at me with a look I can't read. It's wry, almost bitter, but at the same time, it almost seems somehow . . . relieved?

When Noah finally replies, his voice is much calmer. "What a bunch of horseshit. You're reading way too much into this. I already told you why I stopped last night, so quit inventing crazy stories."

I blink, surprised by how much his words sting. *He calls the idea that he might love me . . . a bunch of horseshit?*

But what do I care? I don't love him. Romance was never part of this marriage, and it's not part of our bedroom experiments either. So why does his vehement denial feel so . . . disappointing? I was just trying to get him to acknowledge what Camry and I discussed, that sex between us might seem like a big deal, but it's not. We can keep it casual.

Disguising my twinge of hurt, I reply briskly, "Well, if you're feeling better, then let's reschedule sex for tonight. I already picked up some condoms at the drugstore on my way here this morning." I watch his face carefully. "Unless there's a problem with that?"

He frowns, but says, "Sounds good to me."

"Great. See you at home." I open his door and leave, heading back for my own office. Hopefully I can get some work done now that I've set my personal life straight again.

Chapter Nine

Noah

The conversation with Olivia at work today is still ringing through my ears when I make it home just before five. I skipped out on my last meeting, asking my assistant to cover for me, because I know Olivia will be expecting sex tonight. And I know I need to figure out a way to tell her everything. The contract. The bouncing baby we're supposed to make.

She thought I was scared of having sex because I was worried about feeling something for her. But she's wrong. I already feel a lot for her. I always have.

She was adamant. *Tonight. Sex. Period.* Even picked up some condoms. What the fuck am I going to do? Fake a latex allergy? No way in hell will she buy that. It's such a stupid idea; I can't even believe I'm thinking it. I'm so rattled, so panicked, all sorts of crazy shit is pouring through my head.

I kick off my shoes and stow them in the small

entry closet. Loosening my tie, I head into the bathroom, where I stare at my reflection.

When I signed those papers, it seemed like the right thing to do. Save the company? *Check.* Get a shot with the woman I've always dreamed about? *Check.* And make a baby? No problem, right? But now that this is all happening, it's become *real*, and I'm fucking losing it. Losing my edge.

Just over a week into our marriage and I'm already the world's worst husband. Rosita was right about the dark circles under my eyes. I look like hell. I splash some cool water on my cheeks, hoping it might help. No such luck. I still look confused and tired and scared.

Well, fuck that. I straighten my shoulders. That's not me. I'm not some wimpy little boy who's too afraid to take care of his woman. And that's what this is, isn't it? Olivia has needs. And I'm supposed to be the one to take care of those needs.

I have two choices when Olivia gets home tonight. I can come clean with everything, tell her about the heir clause, show her the section in the contract she missed. Or . . . I can keep my fucking trap shut and go along with what she wants. No-strings sex.

We're just beginning to click. She's just beginning to trust me. If I fuck her tonight and she enjoys herself—which I have no doubts she will—that's a big step toward bringing us closer as a couple. And isn't that what we need if we really are to parent together? I think that's what Rosita was trying to say today, that Olivia and I need to enjoy ourselves. We're in our honeymoon stage of marriage, after all. Baby-making can come later. After our relationship is strong enough that the heir discussion won't bring it crashing down around us.

If safe sex is what she wants, with condoms galore, I'll do it. If I don't, I'll arouse her suspicions. What choice do I have? The only thing I can do for now is buy more time to think. I just need to shut up and do my husbandly duty until I can figure out the best way to broach the topic of babies with her.

Glancing one last time in the mirror, I exhale a deep breath. *Just go with it, man.* This can be good for both of us. It can be the start of something real. For now, my wife wants to be fuck buddies, and I'm sure as hell not turning my nose up at *that* opportunity.

I head into the kitchen and start pulling ingredients out of the fridge to make dinner. I don't know how to make many dishes, but there are still a few Mum taught me that I remember.

Now that I'm in the kitchen, with the soft sizzle of the sauté pan to keep me company, my deception doesn't seem quite the earth-shattering catastrophe I thought it was going to be. I'm not a coward, not really *lying*. I'm just being thoughtful—taking care to choose the right moment to bring up a sensitive topic.

I work efficiently, chopping and dicing as I wait for my wife to get home from work. It all feels so normal, so utterly mundane.

My phone chimes, and I see there's a new text from Olivia.

> OLIVIA: *I'm on my way home. Everything still on plan for tonight? Because we're totally going to fuck. Right, Mr. Tate?*

Reading her dirty words sends a little thrill racing through me. With my heart kicking up speed, I reply.

NOAH: Absolutely. I'm down if you are.

OLIVIA: It's time to put up or shut up. Time to get with the program. And from what I can tell, it's a big program. ;)

NOAH: See you soon, wifey.

I chuckle and set the phone aside to finish dinner.

What the hell was I freaking out about?

This is going to be fun.

Chapter Ten

Olivia

The smell of fish, lemon, and fresh green herbs greets me when I come home. Stepping into the apartment, I inhale deeply and my stomach growls. I quickly take off my work flats so I can check out the kitchen.

I walk in just in time to see Noah bending over to pull a pan of roasted salmon filet and asparagus out of the oven. When he looks over his shoulder at the sound of my footsteps, I try to pretend that I was staring at the food and not his ass.

"Hey, Snowflake, great timing."

"That looks amazing." I swear I just mean the dinner when I say that. "I didn't know you could cook."

With a chuckle, Noah sets the full pan on the counter and turns to pull plates from the cupboard. "Wait until you taste it before you get too excited. I learned how to make baked fish from Mum, and the vegetables and rice from the Internet." He points at a glass dish full of steaming pilaf that I hadn't noticed before.

"Well, it looks good," I chirp, then immediately remember I already said that. Goddammit. I might be freaking out a tiny little bit. I want this, I really do . . . but it's still nerve-racking.

And my butterflies only get worse when Noah glances at me with a catlike half smile, full of sinful promise. "I thought we should ease into things before . . ." He lets his words trail off.

My mind jumps ahead to where he'll be "easing into" later tonight. My stomach jumps with it, and almost without realizing, I wet my lips. Then I yank my eyes away from his.

"I, um, I guess I'll get the drinks," I stammer, sweeping past him with more bustle than strictly necessary.

I find a bottle of chardonnay chilling in the fridge, pour two glasses full, and get the silverware while Noah plates the food. Once the table is set, we take our first bites . . . and a quiet moan of pleasure escapes me.

Our dinner is just as delicious as it looked and smelled. The salmon filets and asparagus are fresh, fork-tender, and lightly seasoned with salt, pepper, and olive oil. The lemon-herb rice perfectly rounds out the meal with its fragrant fluffiness.

"I take it I've earned your seal of approval," Noah teases. "I hope I can hear that sound again later tonight."

I flush slightly, but I'm in too good a mood to tell him to shut up. Teasing him back, however, is something I can manage. "What was with all your false modesty earlier? 'Oh, it might suck, just bear with me . . .'"

He laughs. "I never said it like that. For your information, I *do* like to cook—I just don't usually take the time. And I haven't mastered many recipes. A real man accepts his limitations."

"Evidently a real man also talks in third person." I grin at him. Then my tone sobers. "So, you're still feeling okay? Not sick at all?"

What I'm really asking is *are you ready for sex?* Just without actually having to say that big S-word. And maybe I'm also apologizing for acting like a bitch earlier today, without actually having to say the other big S-word.

He pauses, then gives me a firm nod. "Never better. So I'm still on if you are."

Did his smile slip a tiny bit, or am I just imagining things? I knock back a mouthful of wine to stop myself from overthinking. Tonight is for my body, not my mind. *If he says he's ready to go* . . . I chase the butterflies in my stomach with another bite of rich salmon.

When our plates are empty, Noah suggests, "How about we have another glass of wine?"

So I guess we're not jumping straight into bed. I'm torn between relief and impatience. "S-sure, that sounds nice," I reply.

We refill our glasses and move to the living room. But when we sit down on the couch, Noah doesn't touch his drink. He sets it on the coffee table—and rests his hand on mine. I look up to see his expression has turned predatory.

And just like that, everything changes. The atmosphere, already flirtatious before, darkens and thickens like the air before a thunderstorm.

"Did I ever tell you how hot you look in your office clothes?" he purrs. "Well, really, you look hot in everything . . . and I'm sure you'll look even better in nothing at all." He gives me a lustful smirk. "But we'll get around to that soon enough. Anyway, as I was saying, those clothes are so prim and proper that seeing you at work always gives me . . . ideas."

Fuck, that voice should be illegal. I swallow hard and put down my wineglass before I spill it all over the carpet.

"L-like what?"

"Like kneeling under your desk, my face between your legs, doing my best to distract you while you're on an important phone call." His finger traces over the back of my hand, following the path his tongue would take in his fantasy. "And then, when you make it through the whole call without blowing our cover, you get your reward. I pick you up and fuck you on your desk. Skirt rucked up around your hips, panties pulled aside, blouse open so I can feel your luscious tits pressed against my chest . . ."

I'm speechless. By how hot my face feels, I'm probably also red as a tomato.

Noah continues. "People say only women are attracted to power. That's bullshit. Men are too . . . most of them are just scared of powerful women. But not me." He tightens his grip on my hand and pulls it down to cup his huge, hard bulge, showing me how true his words are. "Rest assured, Snowflake, I'm not going to stop tonight. Not until you're satisfied."

My reply dissolves into a moan as he kisses me hard.

His hand cradles my head, his fingers tangled in my hair, gripping firmly, guiding me where he wants. Where we both want. His other hand caresses me, stroking a long line from my jaw down my neck and then back again. A slow, firm petting that's meant to relax me, open me up to his touches. And it works. Soon I'm melting into him.

As if he can sense the exact moment I'm ready, his fingers drift down to undo my blouse. One button after the other slips free, the pace so leisurely I almost start to squirm. Not wanting him to break our kiss, even just a pause, even to undress me, I wriggle out of my blouse myself. I feel his mouth curve into a small, smug smile against my lips.

His touches transform from soothing into stimulating—teasing the sensitive spot just under my ear, tracing the dip of my spine all the way from my nape to the small of my back. My breath hitches in anticipation every time his fingers bump over the clasp of my bra, wondering if *now* is when he'll undo it. But only when I arch against him does he finally move.

With a single deft movement of his fingers, my band goes slack. My cheeks flush hot and I suppress a tiny squeak of surprise. *Jeez . . . I know he's had a lot of practice with undressing women, but even I can't take off my bra one-handed.*

Noah pulls back to draw the straps down my shoulders, drinking in the sight of my breasts as they're slowly revealed. I shiver, feeling his eyes on me like a physical caress. I'm still wearing my skirt and pantyhose, but Noah's hungry gaze makes me feel so exposed. In a strangely good way, though—not vulnerable or weak. Like he's seeing the real me, undisguised, and I'm the most beautiful thing he's ever seen. The only woman in his world.

Almost worshipfully, he bends his head to kiss my nipple. I suck in my breath; even that light touch zips through me like a static shock. Encouraged, he mouths it again, wetter this time, his lips sliding over the stiffening nub, shooting sparks straight to my clit. I let out a soft, husky moan when he starts sucking and licking—then another when he cups my other breast in one large hand and pinches the nipple.

"W-wait, time out," I gasp. "You're still . . . shirt . . . not fair . . ." It's damn near impossible to string together a sentence under this onslaught.

Smirking, Noah backs off. I take the opportunity to catch my breath while he pulls his shirt over his head and drops it on the floor next to mine.

"You want to take this to the bedroom?" he asks.

I nod emphatically, glad that he saved me the effort of saying it out loud. I want him so badly, my whole body is thrumming.

He takes my hand and leads me down the hall. He sits on the bed, with me standing between his knees, and leans forward to wrap his arms around my waist. As his hands work on unzipping my pencil skirt, his mouth resumes its assault on my breasts. I breathe hard, clutching at his shoulders to keep my balance.

At last the black twill pools on the floor and I step out of it, further into his embrace. Noah's erection brushes my lower thigh. Feeling bold, I push my knee forward to rub against it, and I'm rewarded with a stifled groan. Then it's my turn to groan when Noah cups my crotch firmly.

"Damn," he growls, "you've soaked right through your panties, Snowflake. I could probably get you off right now, just like this."

Suddenly I'm flipped onto my back on the bed, Noah looming over me. "But I won't," he continues. "Because we both know what tonight is about. Some good old-fashioned *fucking*." One finger trails from my collarbone between my breasts, all the way down my body, leaving goosebumps in its wake. I bite my lip as his fingertip ghosts over my pussy lips through the damp fabric of my panties.

He grins like a wolf. "However, we do need to get you nice and wet first."

And with that, before I can say anything, Noah pulls off my panties and dives in. A wild keening cry bursts from my throat. His tongue writhes against my swollen clit and I can barely catch my breath, let alone keep quiet. Jesus, the boy eats pussy like he's dying of thirst. His long, thick finger pushes inside me and curls up and *holy shit, do that again!* My fingers tighten in his hair, shoving his face against my pussy until he probably can't breathe, but I don't care, I can't stop, it's too much and my muscles have locked all on their own.

His finger withdraws, only to return with reinforcements. Little desperate noises escape me as Noah licks my clit and scissors his index and middle fingers deep inside me. I'm actually trembling, and it's not just from the overpowering sensation. I know why he's putting so much effort into preparing me. I've seen his enormous cock before—and it's been a long damn time since I've had anything at all inside me. So I'm going to need all the lubrication and stretching I can get.

A thrill runs down my spine, one part nervousness to ten parts excitement. My stomach clenches with anticipation. I'm so ready for this, for *him*, I feel like I'm on fire. Panting aloud, I quiver and clench around his fingers. *Almost there, almost . . .*

Until the son of a bitch pulls back. "Not yet," he teases.

I almost give him a dirty look for stopping. But I know what's next, and I want to come with him inside me. I nod at him in speechless eagerness as he quickly sheds his pants and boxers, then takes a condom from his nightstand drawer and rolls it on.

Wait, this picture seems wrong. I try to gather my lust-fogged thoughts. He had condoms all along—last night too? Then why did he stop when I mentioned them? And why did I have to go to the drugstore this morning?

But my thoughts dissolve as he starts easing his

cock into me. My breath hitches; he's so thick and it's been such a long time, even the first inch stings a little.

"Wait," I gasp, and he immediately freezes.

"You okay there?"

"Y-yeah," I reply. "Keep going. Just . . . go slow." No way in hell do I want him to stop now. I don't care where the condoms came from, so long as we can just *fuck* already.

Bit by bit, he works his way inside me, pausing whenever I tense up. "Good girl. You're doing so good," he murmurs.

His voice is strained; I'm sure from holding himself back. He looks incredibly sexy poised over me, with his lips parted and those veins standing out in his tensed forearms.

Just when I feel like I can't take any more, at last he bottoms out. I'm already damp with sweat. The feeling of fullness is breathtaking, a slightly burning stretch that balances on a knife edge between pleasure and pain.

He starts withdrawing again, then pushes back in,

just as slowly as before. But I'm ready for the real thing now. I dig my heels into his lower back to urge him on.

His eyes light up. "Oh, that's how it is?"

I moan in response, because forming actual words when he's so deep inside me just isn't possible.

"You're ready to be fucked hard now?" He slowly pulls out, almost all the way—then snaps his hips forward.

My mouth falls open in a silent cry. He rocks back and slams in again and again, finally fucking me in earnest. Bliss crashes through me with every sharp thrust, each wave coming right on the heels of the last, keeping me afloat, drowned, overwhelmed. I'm dizzy with pleasure. It's so intense I can't think or breathe or do anything but whimper.

"Damn, baby, you feel amazing," Noah groans. "I've wanted this for so long. I used to jerk off every night thinking about you . . . wanted to bury my cock in you, make you scream my name. You made me come so fucking hard."

His voice is ragged with need. I feel a thrill at the

idea that I've driven him so wild, made him lose all his control. Noah Tate, the man who can have any woman he wants, has waited years just for me.

He crushes our lips together, his tongue searching for me. The shift in position presses my legs up, and his pelvis grinds against my clit with every move. I moan desperately into his mouth. The waves of ecstasy surge higher and higher—

Until they crest and crash, my release pounding through me. "Noah!" I cry out as I quake apart in his arms.

"Fuck, I can feel you coming . . . so tight, so good, I'm—"

His husky voice collapses into a shapeless growl, a dark, primal sound of pure pleasure. He gives a few more hard thrusts, shuddering into me until his hips slow and finally still.

For a few minutes we just cling to each other, panting for breath, savoring the last aftershocks as we come down from our high. I'm not sure I could get up even if I wanted to. Now I understand what women mean when they talk about feeling the Earth move.

I suck in my breath when Noah eases himself out. He leans over me to throw the condom in the trash, then lies down beside me, his head propped up on his elbow to gaze down at me.

"So . . . what did you think?"

Oh, come on. After all that, he shouldn't expect me to speak coherently, let alone leave a damn Yelp review.

"Good," I mumble. That's the best I can manage. But I guess that's less embarrassing than *eleven out of ten* or *I can't feel my legs.*

I feel his chuckle more than hear it. He reaches for my hand and laces our fingers together. Lifting my hand to his lips, he presses a gentle kiss to the back of it, then pulls to draw my arm over his body.

Held safe in his embrace, I lie limp, exhausted, bathed in a warm golden glow of satisfaction. I finally did it. I fucked Noah Tate, and it was one of the best ideas I've ever had. I knew sex was better than my past experiences—otherwise, people wouldn't talk about it as much as they do—but I never imagined it could be this good. Even my teenage fantasies barely measure up.

I decide that my boring, painful fumbling with Brad didn't count at all. Tonight was my *real* first time. A whole new world of pleasure has opened itself before me, and I intend to explore it to the fullest.

An enormous yawn overtakes me, interrupting my thoughts. *Phew . . . right after I get some rest.*

I wriggle closer to Noah and pillow my head on his bicep. Together, we drift off to sleep.

Chapter Eleven

Noah

Watching Olivia put this cocky asshole in his place is exhilarating.

It's our regular Friday morning executive planning meeting with the board chair, Olivia's father, Fred; my late father's advisor, Prescott; and the department heads from marketing, finance, and HR. Olivia just finished explaining her plan for the upcoming quarter. And the finance executive—a dinosaur named Peter who we should have fired last decade—made the fatal mistake of questioning her expertise a little too adamantly.

"Peter, I appreciate your passion on the topic." Olivia's voice is sure and steady, much calmer than I would have been in her place. "But since Noah and I took over as co-CEOs, this company's performance has steadily improved."

Peter shifts in his chair with a noise that sounds too much like a scoff for my liking.

I frown at him. *Hey, fuck you too, buddy.*

I don't know why it's just now occurring to me, but the prejudices Olivia has faced to take over her corner office and head of the conference table have surely been daunting. She's young, she's a woman, and she's the former boss's daughter—all things that small-minded men like Peter take to assume that she's not qualified for her new role.

I want to throw in my own two cents about his behavior, but I don't. Olivia can handle herself, and I won't imply otherwise by jumping to her rescue, especially not in front of all these company officers. She doesn't need a man to save her, and it's a quality I admire so much about her.

Without missing a beat, Olivia finishes shutting down Peter as if she hadn't heard his scoff. "If you'd like to discuss my plan further, you can join me in my office later and I'll be happy to walk you through it . . . using small words, if it helps. However, I won't let you derail this meeting any further. Now, does anyone have any more business, or are we adjourned?"

Peter's mouth drops open. But he soon closes it

again, defeated, and I suppress a grin.

When nobody else says a word, Olivia rises to her feet. "Thank you all for your time this morning, and please have your department summaries to me by the end of the day."

Everyone scatters until only Olivia and I are standing in the conference room. "Are you okay?" I ask.

She inhales a deep sigh. "Of course."

Even if she wasn't okay, it's in her DNA to put on a brave face and carry on. It makes me proud to know her, to work with her, and to be the man who gets to go home with her.

"Peter's a cocksucker. Come on, let's go get a tea."

She smiles for the first time since the meeting began. "Sounds great."

I lead Olivia to my office, where my secretary was thoughtful enough to get me an electric kettle. A small glass-topped cart holds bottled water, a collection of different English bagged teas, and a couple of mugs.

When the water heats up, I pour Olivia a cup and

hand it to her. She looks at me hesitantly.

"What?" I ask.

"Do you mind if we close the door?"

"Not at all." I walk across the office and shut the door, wondering what the privacy is for.

She sips her tea while I prepare my own cup, then sit down in the armchair next to hers. The late morning sunshine makes everything feel cheery, but I suspect there's something on her mind. She twists the simple diamond and platinum wedding band on her finger.

"Tell me what's on your mind, Snowflake," I prompt her. Something serious is clearly brewing in there, and I suspect it has to do with last night.

We fucked like rabbits and slept naked in each other's arms. Then this morning, we got ready for work and ate breakfast as usual, like none of it ever happened. I have no idea what's going through her head, if she regrets it or what.

My dick definitely wants a repeat performance. Already I've started fantasizing about spending all weekend fucking her brains out. *Hey, a man can hope, right?* But I don't know how she feels about our first time. And to be honest . . . I'm not totally sure how I feel either.

Part of me hoped the sex would be mediocre. That Olivia's cool, collected demeanor would spill over into the bedroom, and she'd be a lifeless lay. Oh, how wrong I was. She was responsive and oh-so-eager for me, matching me thrust for thrust, whimpering sexy mewling cries each time I hit deep inside her.

And when she came? She didn't hold back, like some women do, afraid to be too loud, making sex into something shameful. No, Olivia celebrated it. Crying out with her orgasm, panting my name, clawing my back. I followed her over the edge . . . and now I'm afraid I'd follow her anywhere.

Last night was almost too perfect. Better than any woman I've ever been with. And a deep, dark part of me already knows the reason why. She's special; there's something between us that I've never had before. Even though I've always wanted Olivia, always felt strongly about her, it's jarring to admit just how much she means to me. How hard she makes my heart pound, how far I will go for her . . .

Apparently not enough to man up and tell her about the contract. My stomach tightens.

Olivia sets her mug on the glass table in front of us and crosses her legs. She's in a sexy figure-hugging white dress with a tailored black blazer over the top. A chunky turquoise necklace is the only bright pop of color in her outfit, but it's exactly enough. The woman knows how to present herself. Remembering my thoughts from the meeting earlier, I wonder how much time she spends every morning, finding the perfect balance between feeling feminine and being taken seriously as a professional.

"I, um . . ." She pauses, looking down at her red-lacquered fingernails.

"Tell me." I lean closer.

"Last night was . . ." She trails off again, wringing her hands in her lap. "It was like a bucket list thing. Something to check off my list—no-strings sex with Noah Tate. I thought it'd be fun, and I psyched myself up to just do it."

"And now that we've done it?" My heart starts to pound.

She takes a deep breath.

"Look at me, Olivia." I need to see into her eyes, need to see if she regrets it like I fear she does

She looks up, and the haunting depth in her gaze almost guts me. "Once wasn't nearly enough," she breathes.

In one heartbeat, I've pulled her into my arms, smashing her chest against mine. Her tongue darts out to tease her lower lip just before my mouth crashes against hers.

I need her out of this dress and bent over my desk as soon as fucking possible. Without breaking our kiss, I tug off her blazer and find the zipper at the back of her dress, drawing it down the graceful slope of her spine. Once she's stripped down to just her nude lace bra and thong and her black stiletto heels, I spin her so she's facing my desk.

Placing each of her palms on the desk, I say, "Hold on, baby." Then I drop to my knees behind her and caress her round ass, giving it a playful swat.

She lets out a sharp yelp, more startled than in pain.

"Shh," I tell her, smoothing my hand over the pink stinging spot. "Can you stay nice and quiet for me?"

Olivia nods, her gaze darting over to the door to my office. The very unlocked door where someone can come in at any moment.

I rub her pussy through the damp fabric of her thong and she lifts her ass, rocking her hips against my hand.

"So eager. Promise you can stay quiet?"

She nods again.

I lift the edge of her panties and push one finger into her snug channel. So deliciously tight and hot. I enjoy the view of watching my finger sink in, deeper and deeper, one knuckle disappearing after another, then slowly slide out again. She's already breathing hard, and her inner walls grip me with every move.

Getting married has made me realize something. I don't want an endless parade of one-night stands anymore. I want . . . intimacy. Domesticity. Someone to cook for and cuddle with, someone to share in my triumphs and keep my bed warm at night. I want a wife. I want Olivia.

But once again, a shadow falls over my thoughts. I'm still hiding the truth from her. I don't know how she'll react, how to explain things in a way that protects both her feelings and the company. And as long as I'm deceiving her, I can never have the true connection I'm craving. The secret of the heir clause will be a wall between us. Invisible to her, insurmountable to me.

I give myself a mental shake. Olivia is panting and rocking her hips in time with my motion, desperate for more. What the fuck is wrong with me? Olivia's naked ass and pussy are right in my face and I can't pay attention.

Focus, dumbass, I scream at myself. *Your wife needs you. What kind of man would leave her hanging?*

I withdraw my fingers—oh fuck, her little whimper of disappointment zings straight to my dick—press on her back until she lies flat on the desk with her ass raised, and plant my lips right over her clit. Just one hard suck pulls a wild cry from her lips. With a chuckle, I lean back on my heels.

"Sorry," she whispers. "Please don't stop. I'll behave."

I grin and dive in for more. Planting both hands on her ass cheeks, I part her wet lips with my thumbs so I can reach the spots that make her bite her lip as she fights to stay quiet.

I lick and suck until she's a trembling, writhing mess. I don't let up, mercilessly eating her pussy from behind. My fingers dig into her hips as I press my face harder into her. I need to be deeper. I need to be as close to Olivia as I can get, drowning in her taste and smell and hot, slick feel, and still it's not enough.

She comes with a stifled moan, her chest heaving on my desk. I kiss her ass, her thighs, the back of her knees as she shudders, then rise to my feet.

Instead of thanking me, or making some dry remark like I've come to expect from her, Olivia immediately begins opening the front of my pants. *Hell yeah*. My belt hits the floor and she shoves my pants and boxers down to my knees.

She takes my cock in her hands and starts pumping while kissing my throat. She's so damn sweet, so eager, it's almost too much. I lift her by the hips and sit her on my desk. She's still wearing her thong, but that's no problem.

As she continues to stroke me, I step between her thighs and lift the elastic edge of her panties, pulling them all the way to the side so she's exposed to me.

"Ready for more?" I ask, parting her delicately with my thumbs.

A whimper is the only affirmation I get.

I step closer and rub the head of my cock against her clit. Olivia gasps and looks down between us.

"You're so sexy," I say, rubbing myself along her heat, coating myself in her wetness.

She watches my eyes the entire time. It's a thrill that she can't keep her gaze off mine, but there's something about it that scares me too. Like she's going to see exactly how I feel about her, discover that my feelings for her run much deeper than fake husband and wife. Maybe this is what it means to love someone. It's scary and uncertain, and you're always terrified of fucking it up. But for me, it's not a question of *if* I fuck it up. It's *when*.

Focus, Noah.

I align the head of my cock and press forward the tiniest bit. Just the tip of me has entered her and I stop, realizing we're without a condom. I swallow.

Does Olivia realize it too? Is she okay with this, or did she just not notice? Staying perfectly still, I thumb her clit again. She moans my name.

"Shh, baby." I pet her hair back from her face and kiss her lips.

There's something captivating about this moment. Broad daylight pouring through the window, halogen lights burning overhead. I can see every part of her. It's intimate and illicit, and that's a huge turn-on.

I try to keep from thrusting; I don't want her to cry

out and blow our cover. The frosted glass doors don't block much sound. I'm sure my secretary already heard Olivia when she came.

I follow Olivia's gaze to where it's held captive— the spot where my body joins with hers. Just the flared head of my cock is buried, a thick vein pulsing along the shaft. I stroke her clit again and feel her inner muscles clamp down on me. Pleasure zips down my spine and I'm way too close to coming already.

"Don't fucking squeeze me like that," I growl.

"Shit."

Olivia climbs down off the desk. For a second, I think that she's heard someone—that one of our colleagues, or worse, her father, is about to open the door. But when she doesn't make a move to cover herself, I know that's not it.

"What?" I ask.

"No condom. We can't."

Fuck.

No, scratch that—double fuck.

"Well, this situation . . ." I glance down at my raging erection. "Needs to be taken care of. How can I be expected to work the rest of the day like this?"

She purses her lips. I almost expect her to tell me to suck it up and deal with it. It's what the old Olivia would have done. But this beautiful, sexual creature before me isn't the old Olivia.

"And how do you propose I take care of it, Mr. Tate?"

I love that she's playing right into my fantasy of office sex, complete with calling me by my proper name.

"I could send you on a scavenger hunt for condoms, but that might take too long. Or . . ." I tap my chin thoughtfully.

"Or?"

"I could bend you over my desk and fuck that beautiful ass of yours, or watch you wrap those pretty little lips around my cock and swallow every drop I give you."

Needless to say, the idea of either excites me to no

end.

She looks shy for a moment, just a moment, and I'm dying to know what she's thinking. Then her confidence comes rushing back. "I'm not having the first time we do . . . *that* in your office."

"'That' being back door?" I ask.

She gives me a swift nod.

Interesting. She's not saying never; she's just saying not right now.

My little Snowflake has melted into a puddle for me. Gone is the chilly, no-nonsense woman who I wanted so badly to rustle up. Now she's the woman of my dreams, tough when she needs to be, but soft and eager when we're alone.

Without another word, Olivia drops down to her knees before me and takes me in her hand. Then her mouth is on me and her head is bobbing in time with her hand, and *holy fuck, my wife gives good head.*

After only a minute, I'm panting and my abs are tight, my orgasm close.

"Olivia." I grunt, cupping her cheeks in my hands while she continues bobbing up and down. "I'm going to come."

I warn her to give her a chance to pull away, figuring I'm going to blow my load on the stack of memos on my desk. But her mouth doesn't move, except to swallow me deeper with a sultry moan.

Fuck. I come hard, with blood thundering in my ears, and Olivia swallows every drop.

"Holy hell, princess." I help her to her feet, then tuck myself back inside my pants. "That was incredible."

She gives me a sly grin. "I'm glad you enjoyed it, Mr. Tate."

After a long kiss good-bye, Olivia leaves and I sit down at my desk with a lovesick grin on my lips.

But the peaceful atmosphere is not to last. With a tap on the doorframe, Fred enters.

"Hey, Noah, do you have a minute?"

Reluctantly I nod. *Fuck.* I hope he doesn't notice that it smells like pussy in here. His daughter's pussy.

"Come on in, Fred. What can I do for you?"

"Do you mind if I close the door?" he asks.

I nod. "Of course not." So far his visit is eerily similar to Olivia's, but if he thinks I'm eating his ass on my desk, he's dead fucking wrong.

Once the office door is closed, Fred lowers himself into the armchair in front of my desk. "How are things going?" he asks, his lips pursed and his tone filled with skepticism.

"Fine?" I reply, confused. *What the fuck is he getting at?*

"I actually came to talk to you about something sensitive. Specifically, is Olivia pregnant yet?"

"Um . . ." I swallow and my gaze darts away from his.

"Because Peter's little tantrum in the meeting this morning was only the beginning, I fear."

"What do you mean?" If any of these asshats try to undermine Olivia, if any of them try to come at her in any way, so help me God . . .

Fred shifts uncomfortably in his seat. "The board agreed to ninety days."

"Yes, and?" I tap my fingers impatiently on the desk. We still have plenty of time, by my watch.

"And more than a month has passed without much in the way of results. They're growing restless. They're still entertaining offers to dissolve us, son."

The look in his eyes isn't just uncertainty. It's sheer panic. I let out a heavy sigh.

"And there's something else," he continues. "My health . . ."

"What is it, Fred?" I lean forward in my chair, placing my elbows on the desk.

"Well, I was diagnosed with an aggressive form of cancer earlier this year, as you know. But I've received word from my oncologist that it hasn't responded to treatment as well as we'd hoped."

"Does Olivia know?"

He shakes his head. "Not yet. I hope to try one more treatment before I tell her. And she's got so much on her plate right now."

I nod. I'm not unfamiliar with what it's like to watch a parent die. "I'm going to take care of her, Fred."

He smiles at me sadly. "I know you will." Then he rises from his seat and wanders to the door.

I don't like the slump of his shoulders, the tired defeat in his posture. "Fred, hang in there, buddy. We've got this." I force some hopeful optimism into my voice.

He faces me and nods. "Let's just get a pregnancy test scheduled soon. We need some good news around here."

My mouth goes dry, and I swear I can feel the blood drain from my face. "Soon," I choke out.

"With you two now married, the numbers looking up, and a baby hopefully on the way, the board won't have a leg to stand on. You'll win this fight."

Fred leaves, closing the door behind him. Which is good, because I don't know how I can face anyone right now.

Olivia still doesn't know. The company is still in trouble. Everything is riding on this. But if I come clean to Olivia, tell her that the real reason we got married was to produce an heir, I have good cause to believe she'll walk away forever. And if I don't knock her up, we'll lose our company to a rival firm. It's either lose Olivia . . . or lose Tate & Cane Enterprises.

I lean forward to bury my face in my hands. *Christ.*

What am I going to do?

Chapter Twelve

Olivia

The next week passes in a blur of long hours and stolen moments. On workdays, Noah and I bust our asses at the office, the perfect models of diligent leadership. But we flirt and kiss every chance we get, and we jealously guard our nights together. For the first time in a long time, Tate & Cane isn't the only center of my life—something else has joined it.

At a familiar knock on my open office door, I look up from my computer.

Noah leans against the doorjamb. "Hey there, Snowflake. You hungry?"

"Is that a pickup line, or are you talking about actual, literal hunger?" I reply with one raised eyebrow. *If he asks me whether I want a nice big sausage, I swear to God . . .*

"I'll take whatever I can get." Noah chuckles. "But no, I was just wondering if you wanted to grab lunch soon. I wanted to ask your professional opinion on a couple things."

I consider. On one hand, I'm kind of in the middle of something. On the other, I'm also getting hungry. I check my clock. Sure enough, it's lunchtime. And we'll be talking about business while we eat . . .

Why not? Deciding that this report can wait another hour, I roll my chair back and get up. "I can go right now if you're ready. I actually have some stuff I wanted to ask you about too."

We take the elevator down to the lobby. The weather is nice, so we decide to walk to a small but classy sushi bar about a block from the office. All the way there, we keep finding reasons to touch each other—hands brushing together, hips "accidentally" bumping, playful shoulder nudges, quick affectionate squeezes around the waist.

The hostess seats us at a cozy table for two, tucked away from the window.

Once we have our drinks, I prompt Noah, "So you wanted to ask me something?"

He waves his hand. "You go first."

"Well," I begin, settling back in my chair, "I'm worried about this year's retreat." Normally, we hold a tropical company retreat every winter, and we always invite the executives of our most valuable clients. It's all part of maintaining Tate & Cane's image of personalized, luxury service. "I just don't think we can afford it right now. Even if we can, it'll make things awfully tight . . ."

I expect Noah to object. Or at least make an innuendo about "tight things." Events like this are always huge networking opportunities. And if we deviate from our usual routine, clients might get suspicious about our finances. The last thing we need is a repeat of last month's Red Dog Optics panic.

But Noah surprises me when he replies, "Then let's cancel this year. Our employees will understand, and we can find some other way to butter up our clients."

I blink, iced tea paused halfway to my mouth. "That's exactly what I've been thinking. You read my mind."

By now I've seen his mischievous smirk a million times, but it still sends a subtle tingle down my spine when he purrs, "I hope there's other, more fun things on your mind too."

While I can't help returning his smile, I try to stand firm and stay focused. "Back to our clients—what 'other ways' did you have in mind?"

Thinking, Noah rubs his stubbled chin. "We could invite the execs to a private gala. One day, one night. Even if we pay for their airfare and hotel, it'll be less expensive than sending over a hundred people to Jamaica. We can say something like 'we decided to host a more intimate event this year' so we don't have to admit the real reason."

"Won't they see right through that?" In this kind of context, everyone knows that *intimate* is just a code word for *small*.

Noah shrugs. "What else can we do? If you say we can't afford a retreat this year, then I believe you."

I'm embarrassed to feel a little flutter at his words. He trusts my professional judgment without question. It was such a simple, innocent statement but it carries so much weight, so much faith.

"And we have to place the same kind of trust in them to see us for what we really are," Noah continues. "You never know . . . if we really want to transform Tate & Cane, honesty might turn out to be our greatest strength. A smart client would appreciate our frugality and efficiency." He winks at me. "And don't worry, I'll still show them a great time, budget or no budget. They won't miss the Caribbean one bit when I'm through with them."

"Okay, sure. I'll leave it to the master party animal." Sipping my drink, I wave my hand. "Looks like we have a consensus. Motion passed. Now it's your turn."

He says, "I've been debating whether to pitch our new service style to Acentix Telecom. They're kind of old-fashioned . . ." One of the few regulars that Dad and Bill managed to hang on to over the years, in fact. "And they've always been happy with our work in the past."

"So you're wondering, should we even bother

trying to update them?" I clarify.

"Right. I figured you'd say, 'If it ain't broke, don't fix it.'" He turns his palms up. "But I thought I'd ask anyway."

I stare into my glass as I weigh our options. Noah knows me well; my first instinct is to avoid spending resources on non-vital work. Pulling together a pitch meeting won't take a huge amount of effort, but it's not very likely to yield much of a return either.

For some reason, though, I'm feeling bold. Something inside me whispers *why not?* And that voice sounds a lot like Noah.

The man himself sips his drink and watches me, keeping quiet, giving me all the time I need to think.

Finally, I reply, "I think we might as well try. At worst, Acentix says 'no, thanks'—which is always a risk when pitching anyway—and we continue the services we've been providing them all along. So why not? The whole reason Dad made us co-CEOs is so we could shepherd this company into the digital era, right? We shouldn't be shy about trying new things."

Noah smiles, locking eyes with me. "Experimenting with new things has sure worked out pretty well for us."

The meaningful glance we share is broken by a ding from Noah's phone. He checks it, his smile fading away with every second his dark eyes scan back and forth across the screen.

"What is it?" I ask.

Please no shitstorms for at least another half hour. I know it's a bit selfish of me, since this lunch is for business and not pleasure anyway, but I'm irritated that my one-on-one time with Noah is being interrupted.

"Just an e-mail from our Parrish Footwear project leader," he grumbles. "Don't worry, it's not an emergency. Apparently Estelle has been making noises about how long we're taking to finish their first round of deliverables." Noah gives a wry twist of his full lips. "Even though she was fine with our proposed deadline when she signed the contract."

"We're not liable for late work if it's not actually late. So, legally, our ass is covered. But . . ." I chew my lip thoughtfully. "We should probably still try to smooth her feathers. This relationship could make us a lot of money in the long run." And if working with Noah has taught me anything, it's that there's more to maintaining good vibes than just what's on paper. "You should pay Estelle a visit. Invite her to a business lunch, bump into her at a party, something casual like that. Just smooth things over and reassure her about our progress."

Noah blinks, surprised. "You'd really be okay with that?"

"She likes you. We might as well put that rapport to good use." Not too long ago, I would have dismissed this kind of elbow-rubbing as a waste of time. But it's hard to argue with the effectiveness of Noah's charismatic approach.

He cocks his head and I realize what he's really asking.

"Besides, I know nothing would ever happen between you two," I say, smiling warmly at him. A flash of something daring prompts me to add, "She can look all she wants, but only *I* get to touch."

Noah gives a low, pleased noise that's half chuckle and half murmur. "Damn right. By the way, Snowflake, I like this side of you. Any chance of that touching happening anytime soon?"

I return his smoldering stare. "If you play your cards right."

He stretches in his chair with a stifled groan, offering me a tantalizing hint of the taut body under his suit, then leans back with arms crossed over his broad chest. His smirk tells me that he knows exactly what he was doing. "Well, that's the last item on my agenda. You have anything else?"

Sipping my drink, I shake my head. "Not really anything pressing. Camryn asked me the other day about how we should bill content marketing. But I just offered my opinion and let her make the final decision."

Noah's eyebrows quirk. "You, delegating?"

"Her team got the in-depth social media training, not me," I reply with a casual shrug. "And she's handling everything great so far."

But I know why he's surprised. I've finally managed

to chill out and hand over the reins—at least, where my loyal, responsible BFF is concerned. Other than giving feedback on her weekly reports, I'm making an effort not to butt in.

"That was easy. All our issues discussed and our food hasn't even arrived yet." Noah grins at me. "Looks like our business lunch will be just a regular lunch."

"Was this your plan all along?" I scold him without any real force. "To get me out on a date with you in the middle of the workday?"

His innocent shrug is spoiled by the fact that he hasn't stopped smiling. "Maybe."

I pause for a long moment, pretending to think hard. "Well . . . I guess I can forgive you."

Noah holds up a finger in protest. "Hey, you're going off script. You're supposed to be mad at me, and then I have to soften you up—"

"In front of the whole restaurant?"

His grin darkens into absolute sin. "Oh, Snowflake, you've got a dirty mind. All I had planned was a kiss.

But I like the way you think, and I seem to remember you not being shy about fooling around in restaurants."

"This is why I like you better when you don't talk," I retort with a smile. *Especially when it's because your mouth is otherwise occupied.*

"So, what's the verdict on my brilliant plan?"

"Hmm . . ." I pretend to ponder again. "I'll take that kiss now. More later."

"At the office?" he asks immediately.

Actually, that doesn't sound so—

Wait, no, what am I thinking? He's dragging me down a rabbit hole. We already crossed that line, and as exhilarating as it was, I don't want to get caught in some scandal.

I give him a firm shake of my head. "At home. Where we can be as loud and take as long as we want."

He heaves a purposely melodramatic sigh. "But that's such a long wait, and you're the one who brought up sex in the first place." Before I can tease him for being a perpetual horndog, he adds, "I guess I can be good for a little longer, though. You're worth waiting for."

My cheeks turn pink even before he leans across the table and his lips brush against mine. I'm not sure how to respond. Sexy flirting is one thing, but that comment was almost too sweet. Too real.

Our lunch chooses that moment to arrive. We dig into the delicious sushi and let ourselves talk about anything but business. All too soon, we'll have to get back to the office, but for now, we savor each other's company. A precious hour alone together, away from the hustle and stress.

• • •

At least once a month, Camryn and I try to set aside some girl time to pamper ourselves and catch up with each other. Today is that most sacred of days. We've booked a luxury pedicure at our favorite salon. We sit side by side in adjacent spa chairs, our long-suffering feet freed from high heels and soaking in warm, lavender-scented whirlpool baths. *Ahh* . . .

"So, how've you been lately?" Camryn asks me as

the attendant massages exfoliating salt scrub into her soles. "Do anything cool without me?"

"Actually, yeah." My tone slips into a soft fondness. "Noah and I spent all of last weekend together. On Saturday we had brunch, went shopping at the farmer's market—he bought me the peonies I always get, without even needing to ask—and then we went to the MOMA's special Impressionist exhibit. On Sunday, we saw *P.B. and Jay*—"

"That new indie rom-com?" she asks, interrupting.

"Yeah. And then we ate dinner out and went dancing."

Feigning shock, Camryn presses her free hand over her heart. "Hang on. I need a minute to process this. Noah Tate, buying flowers and watching chick flicks? And Olivia Cane—"

"But you have no problem imagining Noah at an art museum?"

"At least the paintings probably had naked ladies in them. But Noah Tate, acting so cute and mushy? And Olivia Cane, taking an entire weekend off? Unplanned?

For *fun*? I think I might have a heart attack."

I snort despite myself. "Oh, shut up. I'm not that boring."

"Yes, you are. Tell me something—you sneakily answered work e-mails while he was in the bathroom, didn't you?"

"For your information, I had my phone turned off the whole time we were out."

Camryn's mouth drops open and she twists to face me fully, her shock now genuine. "Holy shit. Who are you and what have you done with my best friend?"

I shrug sheepishly. "Noah convinced me that the office would survive two measly days without me. And I actually . . . believed him."

Camryn says nothing. She just smirks at me like she knows something I don't. My stomach stirs with nervous flutters.

"What?" I finally ask. I know full well I'm taking her bait, but I don't care enough to let her keep up her smug staring.

"Oh, nothing," she says in a singsong voice, her tone soaked with false innocence. "I guess he must be pretty convincing, is all."

"What's that supposed to mean?" I huff. "It's just because I've been more confident about work lately. I feel like Tate & Cane is really starting to get back on track."

"Sure, but business isn't the only thing that's going well. You practically glow when you talk about Noah. And it seems like his free-and-easy ways have rubbed off on you."

The double entendre isn't lost on me but I ignore it, determined to be the more mature woman in the room. "It was just one weekend off. Big deal."

"Yeah, you guys are definitely in your honeymoon phase," she concludes, ignoring me right back. She heaves a sigh of satisfaction that definitely didn't need to be so theatrical. "I had my doubts at first, but it looks like the manwhore can step up and be romantic when he sees something he really wants."

"What are you talking about? He's wanted women

before." Noah practically treated chasing pussy like another full-time job, in fact.

Camryn shakes her head. "Not the same way he wants you. He seems really motivated to win you over. Like, for real. Not just for the company's sake."

My heart gives a little kick. I instinctively start to argue with her. "I'm sure he just . . ."

But then I stop because I realize that his efforts are sincere. To be honest, I always knew they were. And his romantic gestures didn't slack off after we were married or after we slept together. So this can't just be about the contract or the company's public image, or even just about getting into my pants. From the beginning, Noah made no secret of being attracted to me, but lately the atmosphere between us seems like more than just sexual tension.

The attendant interrupts my stunned musings. "Would you ladies like me to apply any nail polish today?"

Wow, I must have been really spacing out. I didn't even think of picking out a color.

"Pale pink," I blurt, feeling playful. Very different from my usual palette of dark matte red, which feels professional and mature for the male-dominated office. Pastel pink, in a way, symbolizes my newly awakened soft side. I smile to myself, wondering what Noah will think.

"Can I see what new shades you have?" Camryn asks.

"I'll bring you our color book," the attendant says as she bustles out of the room.

I sink back into my thoughts. Can Noah actually have serious feelings for me? And if he does, what will I do with this information? How do *I* feel about Noah? I'm having fun now, but is he really long-term husband material?

As much as I've denied it just now, Camryn is right—Noah is changing my routine. Hell, he's changing *me*. The old Olivia never would have let her hair down like I did last weekend. And we're so much more in sync at the office. Not too long ago, we struggled to mesh our management styles, but now we effortlessly work together to solve problems with the easy grace of a rehearsed dance. We've grown across the gap to meet each other halfway.

Almost without my noticing, Noah has become one of my guiding stars. Someone I look forward to seeing each and every day. His smile alone has the power to speed up or slow down my heart. I've been so much calmer and happier lately . . . although that might just be a side effect of having multiple screaming orgasms every night.

As if Camryn can read my mind, she asks in an undertone, "So, have you two done the deed yet?"

Caught off guard, I look away, stammering, "Um . . ."

"Oh my God, you *did*," she says with a squeal. "I'm so proud."

Even though I'm staring intently at the wall, I can still hear the gleeful grin in her voice. My face feels hot.

"You're being weird," I protest.

"Are you kidding? You've finally broken your dry spell. Now I'm not the only one holding up the 'sexy gossip' end of our friendship. I want to hear everything. Hurry up and spill before the attendant comes back." When I stay tongue-tied, she eggs me on. "Is his dick as big as the rumors say?"

"You're unbelievable," I say, groaning in defeat. "Yes, okay? He's huge. Are you happy now?"

"Not until you tell me what he's like in bed."

I may never remove my eyeballs from this wall ever again. "Um . . . let's just say he knows what he's doing."

She gives me a look. "No, let's *not* just say that. Come on, Liv, I need more details!"

"Well, he's . . . assertive. Passionate, but sweet. Very attentive. Sometimes he likes to tease. He takes things slow—" I think my face might burst into flame. "Until he suddenly doesn't."

Camryn gives a little whoop. "Get it, girl!"

Mortified, I frantically wave my hands back and forth. "Jesus, Camryn, keep it down. Half the salon can probably hear us."

But I'm laughing with her even as I try to shush

her. It seems that nothing can put a dent in my sunny mood. My heart is filled to the brim with hope—both about work and about my relationship with Noah.

Camryn opens her mouth, probably to keep grilling me. But I'm saved from further interrogation when the attendant returns with a small binder.

"Sorry about the wait, honey, someone else was using it," she chirps.

As Camryn mulls over the color swatches, I pull my phone out of my purse to text Noah.

OLIVIA: *Almost done at the spa. Going to pick up more condoms on the way home. Want me to get anything else?*

On playful impulse, I add:

OLIVIA: *Like maybe some whipped cream or chocolate sauce?*

Then I hit SEND, grinning foolishly to myself. I'm bubbling over with a joyful, sexy energy I've never felt before. I feel like everything in my life is finally coming together.

A few minutes later, my phone dings with a new message.

NOAH: *Hell yes. You know how much I love dessert, Snowflake.*

I stifle a giggle. God, I'm acting like a silly schoolgirl and I don't even care. If these past few weeks with Noah are anything to go by, I have a lot more fun and games to look forward to.

Chapter Thirteen

Noah

All day I've been delving into Tate & Cane's financial situation, poring over dense, dry records. But I'm home now, and at the cheery sight of Olivia fresh from the spa, smiling at me as she stands in front of my chair, all my stress dissolves.

Well, almost all of it. Fred's e-mail about the possibility of us having to either take out a loan to continue paying employee salaries or consider a mass layoff is still on my mind. Not to mention my promise to Olivia that we'd find a way to wow our clients with an intimate party. And Fred's news about his cancer resisting treatment. And the heir clause, looming over everything . . .

Fuck me running. I tuck the stacks of dreary bank statements into my leather portfolio and close it.

"What do you think?" Olivia grins at me, wiggling her painted toes.

"Pink. I like it." Then again, I'd probably like her in just about anything. I already know I love her in nothing at all.

She smiles at me. "I was feeling flirty."

"Did you have fun?"

Blushing a little, she looks down at the plush carpeting. "Yes, except . . ."

"What is it?"

I rise and pull her chin up so she'll meet my eyes. I hope she hasn't seen our current financial picture yet. She's got enough stress to juggle right now. I've tried to shield her from most of it, asking Fred and Peter to come directly to me with their reports and concerns.

"Camryn grilled me on *us*," Olivia says softly.

Oh. I'm relieved to hear it's nothing related to work. But it's crazy to think there's actually an *us*. I didn't know if we'd ever get to this point.

I shrug. "That's not so bad, right? Things are good between us. Hopefully that's what you told her."

She looks up, her cheeks still hot. "I did. But she wanted to know *specifics*. Like how you were in bed."

A slow smile uncurls on my lips. "And what did you tell her?"

She chews on her lip, looking unsure.

"The truth, Olivia," I say firmly. It's unlikely that she said anything to hurt my reputation—she's polite like that, and besides, I know I'm good. I just want her to tell me how I make her feel. I want to hear those words straight from her soft, full lips.

"That you have a big . . . b-boy parts," she stutters, "and you're . . . assertive, yet tender, and—"

I can't wait another second to have her mouth on mine. I take her mouth hungrily, and her lips part, accepting me. Our tongues duel as I pull her close, chest to chest.

I'm not sure how or when it happened, but she's become mine. She's the first thing I think about when I wake, and the last on my mind before I drift off to sleep. And before I can contemplate the ramifications, I know that I'm going to do what needs to be done to protect my future with her.

Tonight. I need to do it tonight.

I lift Olivia in my arms and carry her toward the bedroom, our mouths still moving eagerly together. Unable to even wait until we reach the bed, I stop in the hall, pinning her back against the wall with her legs wound around my hips.

She's wearing a simple cotton sundress, and that means when I slide my hand along the outside of her thigh and under her ass cheek, I can reach all the way around to the damp center of her panties. Slipping my fingers under the elastic, I find her clit and rub in circles, pulling a moan from her lips that I quickly swallow with another kiss.

It's insane to think that the man who once refused to let a conquest sleep in his bed now shares a home with his wife, and practically attacks her at the door after only a couple of hours apart. Damn, I've turned into a total mushy prick. But there's something so addictive about this woman. The way she carries herself, her wit and intelligence, her insatiable appetite for me. It just feels right.

I've never even been in a serious relationship. According to Sterling, getting married—tied to one woman for all of eternity—should have scared me shitless. Instead, it's made me loyal, faithful, loving. It's brought me to life in all the best ways.

I only hope that doing what I need to do tonight doesn't destroy everything.

"Yes," Olivia cries. She grips my shoulders and rocks her hips into my hand, already getting closer.

I love how she keeps herself bare for me. Running my fingers over her silky center, I ease one in slowly. But my careful pace isn't to last, because when Olivia groans and murmurs my name, I add a second finger and thrust in harder. I finger-fuck her against the wall, my cock so hard it aches. But getting off is the last thing on my mind. I'm content to kiss Olivia and watch her fall apart right here in my arms.

"Noah . . ." She moans, pushing her hands into my hair. "I want you."

"You have me, baby." I kiss the side of her neck, inhaling her honeysuckle perfume as my fingers continue stroking. That familiar scent, so uniquely Olivia, always gets me worked up and calms me at the same time.

"Inside me. I want you inside me when I come."

Okay, then. That changes things. *My baby wants the dick, then the dick she shall have.*

Still supporting her weight with one arm around her hips, I reach between us and undo my jeans, shoving them down enough to free my cock. Then I line myself up, rubbing the head of my cock through her wet folds just to feel her shudder in my arms.

"How's that feel?" I tease her again, dragging the length of myself through her heat, grinding against her oversensitive clit.

"Need you," she moans brokenly.

It's almost hard to believe this is the same woman who a mere month ago turned up her nose at the thought of sex. Thought it was some useless, vile affair that had no place in her busy life. I'm not an egomaniac, but I'd like to believe the reason is *me*. I alone bring out this side of her, make her crazy with desire, unleash her inner sex goddess. Which is fine, because she does the same to me. I crave her like I've never craved anything before.

"Come on." Olivia groans. "Fuck me, Noah." She grips my biceps and watches me with a desperate expression. The need in her eyes is almost painful.

I press forward, the first few inches of me disappearing inside her.

"Wait . . ."

I pause. "What is it?"

"The condoms. They're by the bathroom sink. In the drugstore bag."

Fuck that. "It would feel so fucking good to have you bare." I groan, pushing my hips up so she can feel my hard length between her legs. "My hard cock sliding into your warm, tight heat . . . Please, baby . . ."

"Noah." She groans, her head dropping back. "Not until I'm on birth control."

My stomach drops. Right. Like that'll help.

"Hurry," she murmurs with a final kiss to my lips before shimmying down my body until her feet touch the floor.

I inhale a deep breath and head for the bathroom. Stopping in the doorway with my cock jutting straight out in front of me, I catch my reflection in the mirror and don't like what I see. There's a haunted look in my eyes that wasn't there before.

"Noah?" Olivia calls from the bedroom.

"Just give me a minute." Crushed by rising panic and guilt, I close the door behind me.

Fred's ominous warnings ring in my head. I thought I'd be able to convince Olivia by now, but I haven't even managed to broach the subject with her yet, and we're running out of time. My father's legacy, Fred Cane's dying wish, all of Tate & Cane's employees . . . everything is at stake. I know I have to act, but how?

I grab one of the condoms from the counter. My erection, despite the stress swirling through my brain, hasn't gotten the memo. I stare down at the little foil packet in my hands.

What in the fuck am I doing? I feel utterly lost and confused. I'm falling in love with Olivia, more with every passing day . . . all while hiding the world's biggest secret from her. Despite all our hard work, the company finances are so dismal, we're still barely hanging on. A baby would solve so many problems. Tying up that last loose end of the contract would cement our inheritance and ensure that the board doesn't sell our company out from under us, leaving us destitute—along with six thousand other people.

But Olivia will never agree to that. Hell, she'll probably flip out and call off our whole arrangement if I tell her the truth. I've been racking my brain for weeks, trying to find the perfect sales pitch that will save everything I care about, and I just keep hitting the same brick wall.

I've always been so good with words, and now they've deserted me. Even if I knew what the fuck to say, the right moment never seems to come. And I can't fight off the creeping terror that maybe . . .

Maybe it never will.

Maybe this conversation—this entire situation—

really is impossible. Maybe there is no solution.

The thought makes me go numb. Moving on their own, my hands rifle through the vanity's drawers and cabinets. I don't know what I'm looking for until my fingers brush against it. My mother's sewing kit. The little silver case she gave me the year before she died, when she taught me how to sew a button back onto my favorite shirt.

I pull out a needle and look down at its glinting sharp point. I test the end on my finger and feel its bite. A tiny red droplet wells up, grows rounder, heavier, until it rolls down my finger, leaving a vivid trail, but I still don't move. I just stare stupidly at the stained needle tip. Silver shining through a film of red.

I feel like I'm in a dream—one of those nightmares where you can't run fast enough, like trying to wade through quicksand. My heart is slamming against my rib cage. What the fuck am I doing? Am I really . . . can I ever even *think* . . . ?

A gasp of shock pulls my focus to the door.

Olivia stands naked on the threshold, her mouth

hanging open. Her wide-eyed disbelief quickly plummets into horror. She stumbles back, bumping into the wall behind her, her hand pressed to her mouth like she's about to be sick.

I look down at my hands—one holding a condom, and the other, a needle. With a spasm of disgust, I throw the condom and needle into the sink.

"Olivia . . . w-wait, it's not, I wasn't . . . !" My voice is hollow, unconvincing even to me.

A sob of pain tumbles from her open mouth. When I look back up, my wife is running away, her lovely face twisted with betrayal.

Not knowing what else to do, I follow her, hoping it's not already too late . . . and knowing that it is.

Hitched Volume 3

I've ruined everything. I've broken the cardinal rule and fallen in love with my fake wife, and then I went and did the worst thing a husband can do. Winning her back will be nearly impossible, but I've never backed down from a challenge before and I'm sure as hell not about to start now. Olivia will be mine, and I can't wait to put a bun in her oven.

You won't want to miss the final installment in Noah and Olivia's love story, and especially the way this over-the-top alpha male wins over his bride once and for all.

Acknowledgments

I would like to thank the following ladies who played an important role in helping me bring *Hitched* into the world: Alexandra Fresch, Hang Le, Natasha Gentile, Rachel Brookes, Danielle Sanchez, and Pam Berehulke. I'm so grateful to have each of you on my team.

A big thank-you to Crystal Patriarche and the BookSparks Team. I'd like to give a shout-out to the Cuties in my private Facebook Group, Kendall's Kinky Cuties, and say thank you for cheering me on and being my go-to place when I want to steal a few minutes away and hang out online.

And to John. Always John.

About the Author

A *New York Times*, *Wall Street Journal*, and *USA TODAY* bestselling author of more than twenty titles, Kendall Ryan has sold more than a million e-books, and her books have been translated into several languages in countries around the world. She's a traditionally published author with Simon & Schuster and Harper Collins UK, as well as an independently published author.

Since she first began self-publishing in 2012, she's appeared at #1 on Barnes & Noble and iBooks charts around the world. Her books have also appeared on the *New York Times* and *USA TODAY* bestseller list more than two dozen times. Ryan has been featured in such publications as *USA TODAY*, *Newsweek*, and *In Touch Weekly*.

Other Books by Kendall Ryan

The Gentleman Mentor

Sinfully Mine

ALPHAS UNDONE Series:

Bait & Switch

Slow & Steady

IMPERFECT LOVE Series:

Hitched Volume 1

Hitched Volume 2

Hitched Volume 3

STAND-ALONE NOVELS:

Hard to Love

Reckless Love

Resisting Her

The Impact of You

Screwed

Monster Prick